To Hold a Flower

Caroline Sophia Hamel

Written by Caroline Sophia Hamel

ISBN: 9780578928722
LCCN: 2021911300

Cover art by © Sophia Lindstrom
Edited by © I.O. Scheffer

First printing edition 2022

For my mom and my sister, my best friends, who I love more than anyone and the world. My mom, with whom I have learned to grow and create a truly genuine relationship in which I can be vulnerable and open. We have gone through so much and grown together. I know how much you love me, and I will never let go again. I know you are and always have been there for me. You brought the best out of me, and I am so grateful that you're my mom. I am proud of you for growing with me, growing in yourself, discovering what you want, and being such an amazing person with so much kindness.

My sister, who is the most supportive person in my life. You have grown into such an amazing person, who is so thoughtful, calming, grounding, and the most mature person I know. Honestly, you have developed into such a stunning person that can see and be so much. I have mostly been close with you, and we have always gotten along, despite how different we may have been at times and sometimes we drifted far enough apart that we hardly knew each other, but I am grateful too that I can finally feel like I know the real you and I hope you feel like you know me. You have given me someone to lean on, who cheers me up and brightens my day with such ease. I am sorry that my words have not always come easily and might not always, but I treasure our relationship as siblings and best friends.

I am so grateful to have you both in my life and I love you more than anything.

A Brief Guide to Pronunciation

ie – Used in a name, pronounced as a hard E and then a soft e (Liela is Lee-ell-uh)

y – Used in a name, pronounced as a soft i (Myllia is Mill-ee-uh)

u – Used in a name, pronounced as a hard U (Dunet is Dune-et or Dew-net)

ei – Used in a name, pronounced as you would pronounce air, heir, or their (example – Veir)

Trigger Warning:

Internalized Ableism & Ableism

~

As someone who self-identifies as neurodivergent (an umbrella term for mental disabilities), I now realize that I wrote much of my own shame, guilt, repression, and fear into this book. This ableism is both directed inwards by my main characters and towards a side character, who represents the neurodivergent traits I try to hide. I understand if this is too upsetting to read.

Please read "A Note on Neurodivergence" (right before the "About the Author" section) for further clarification on the neurodivergent rep in this book and a discussion of my future intentions.

Additional Trigger Warnings:

Depictions of Depression & Anxiety

I loved her from the moment she came into my life

Dunet

My sister and my best friend

She is ... the flower that guides me

The flower that I desperately cling to

But sometimes we cling too hard

When we accept that sometimes we need to let go of the fragile images we clutch to our hearts

And learn to grow alongside those we love the most

For that is the purest love

And the purest heartache

To mend and to heal

To strengthen and build

And to embrace those rooted fears of change

For love is something that grows

Something you must choose to grow with

Embracing the true beauty

Of yourself

And those you love

Caroline Sophia Hamel

Your darkness is not a cage

No matter how much you seek to sink into it

You must always break free

Looking for a future that is bright and always there

Waiting for you

For you are beautiful

And someday you will love yourself for all that you are

Pushing forward into a future full of hope

Full of dreams

And full of love

You are never alone

And you never will be

You deserve the world

And to grow into the beautiful person I know you are

You are a scattered leaf in the wind

Unsure and timid

Yet you are here

Kind and capable

Ready to bring this world so much brightness

You will embrace your confidence

Your strengths

And move forward into a steady world

Waiting to receive your touch

Part 1

~ Part 1 ~

Caroline Sophia Hamel

Caroline Sophia Hamel

A Purpose in Joy

Liela

I feel a warm flutter in my chest as I ride home, my patrol behind me, knowing that I would see my sister's beaming face.

We pull into the city gates and then down the wide thoroughfare of quaint, simple housing and bustling shops below the low din of the blustering wind. I resist the urge to shield my face, my eyes keen on the castle in the distance, marking my home.

I pull ahead of my contingent, trying not to appear too eager as my eyes rest on the horizon.

Vel's hooves platter over the cobbles, mixing up the steady flow of dust.

The last traces of summer are vanishing. In a few months it will be snowing here again, and the Kalltarris Mountains set as a backdrop to this city—Claralis, will be covered in a thick blanket of snow.

We stand as the stronghold of Mathar's defenses, the Kalltarris Mountains a steady shield and border to Arathulen. Even with a lasting peace between us, Claralis is a necessary fortress.

This is my father's city and I feel a surge in my chest just knowing that. This is my home, and I will defend it as a promise to all the people I hold dear—my sister, my father, my mother, my friends: Driena, Darnor, and Myllia, as well as my people, and my fellow soldiers. I intend to lead our armies someday and that is a goal that I have and always will strive towards, until I make that dream a reality.

I scan my contingent, briefly meeting Driena's intelligent gaze—silver-flecked, river-blue eyes. Her hair is tied in a ponytail, and she holds her head high, in a graceful manner. Her face is thin, which pairs well with her slender build. She rides near my side, acknowledging me with a brief, gentle smile. My mind feels steady with the knowledge that I have her in my contingent; she is one of my oldest friends and I can always rely on her honesty, resilience, and kindness when I need to.

I cast my eyes over the rest of my patrol. My heart beats steadily as I feel a general sense of ease emanate from them. I hope that, one day, I will truly lead them.

I always admired this city and my father. He is a kind ruler—good to his people. That I know with a sureness in my heart.

More than anything though, this is home. And more than anything else that I yearn for while I am gone is my sister – beautiful and joyful, she will forever cast a smile on my face.

I continue to let the low clatter of Vel's footfalls bring me into a sense of ease, as my fingers lightly press against the reins in anticipation. Not a worried anticipation, just an expectant one, bordering on the light padder in my chest.

But I never let that overwhelm me. I can wait, letting my heart fall muted and slow for now, a prelude to the swell I know will come, as I picture the wonderful tug of Dunet's upturned face. Right now, I am still leading this patrol ... but soon enough I will see her ...

The housing thins out, coming to an abrupt halt as we get near the outer castle wall and move through the arch into the opening lawn.

I pull on the reigns, moving Vel towards the stables and then pausing to turn my head in the direction of the castle steps.

I feel a small burst in my heart as a tiny speck runs out to greet me and gradually grows into the youthful energy of my sister, a palpable ball of joy and optimism – her small frame and fair skin peek from under her silken white dress. Her sapphire eyes look at me in delight, alight and curious, her mouth set in a beautiful smile, showing the small teeth of a carefree child, and her soft, buttery hair is tucked back behind her ears, small and delicate. I can see the clear dimples on her rosy cheeks, and I break out in my own smile.

She stops beside my horse, staring up at me as she holds her hands behind her back.

"I made this for you, Liela!" her voice peaks in a squeal.

I feel a skip in my heart as her hands come from behind her back, presenting me with a crown of daisies.

"Is this for me?" I ask, light filling my heart. She nods her head vigorously and I reach out to take it with a delicate reverence. I look down at her gently. "Thank you, Dunet; it looks beautiful!" In a fluid movement I dismount and embrace her, feeling her small warmth once again. There's a contentment to be home again after days with my patrol.

Dunet beams at the compliment.

"I hope I wasn't gone too long," I say, searching her face as a small pit forms in my chest.

"No!" she clamors. "I spent the day in the courtyard. That is where I found the flowers. I wanted to spend it with mom and dad, but mom was off all day and dad was busy. He had such a large pile of papers!" Her voice turns shrill, her eyes going wide. "It was huge! He said it was important."

"And I am sure that it was." I soften my voice, a tenderness underlying my pupils, both at my sister and for my father. I feel torn knowing she was alone yet again. But as much as it crushes me, I cannot help but smile at her optimism.

"Liela." She looks up at me with luminous eyes and then behind me to Vel, my horse. "Can you take me riding someday?" Her question comes off a little timid. "It is painfully boring without you here."

"I would love to, Dunet." My voice rises into a gentle brush. "You know, I was thinking of taking you and I have a present for just that occasion."

"Really?" She bounces on her heels.

"Really, but you will have to wait just a little, Dunet. I have to finish a few things, first," I say, parsing my lips at the slight ache in my heart. As much as I love her, my schedule always seems to preclude her. "I promise to join you for dinner, later tonight."

Dunet's face lights up. "I cannot wait! Come on, I have an idea! We can make mom and dad dinner!" There's such an enormous energy to her words.

I feel a similar energy flood into me at the prospect of making dinner with my sister. "That sounds like a wonderful idea!" It always puts a smile on my face, spending time with Dunet, and knowing that keeps me going at times when I feel overwhelmed.

I follow her as she prances up the castle steps. She casts her gaze back at the top, stopping to wait for me, her eyes seeming to wander and then flit to me. I crest the steps and take her hand gently, to which she goes calm, her eyes resting on me. I try to ignore the nagging feeling I have and act like I don't see her hesitation. It does weigh in my mind just a little, but I convince myself that it's nothing, just a passing moment.

She looks at me with wide eyes, then turns with a grin, pulling at my hand, to which I follow, picking up my step to fall alongside her. The entryway opens up, fairly high, but nothing overly grand. It stands as a formal waiting area and we pass through it in a short rush, moving into the opening of corridors on the other side. Clean and neat and assigned more to practical spaces on the inside, most of the décor rests in the surrounding courtyards, and arches between the walls reach out to the exterior.

I stop at the bottom of the stairs to our suite, letting go of Dunet's hand and motioning for her to go on without me.

She rests there for a moment, her mouth falling ever slightly, before she turns and climbs the steps.

I head towards the kitchen in a stride, making a point not to take long, still feeling that longing to rejoin my sister.

I stop at the edge of the room, a savory aroma hitting my nostrils as I observe the bustle of the castle kitchen. A few of the staff lower their heads respectfully before Chef Feln appears shortly after, plain-looking, red-haired, and with a pleasant, broad smile.

"Lord Cordre," he inclines his head. "How may I help you?"

"Chef Feln," I say with a light formality. "I thought it pertinent to let you know that Dunet and I will be preparing a meal for your lord tonight and there is no need to cater to us this evening. Dunet is very excited about it." I keep it quite short, but I feel a familiarity with much of the staff, even if I still maintain a necessary distance for an air of respectability.

"Of course, Lord Cordre," Feln replies with a bow, before looking up, a smile playing across his lips. "Lady Dunet has been enjoying her time quite well in our kitchens. She must have something ambitious planned for tonight's meal."

"I know she does." I let my posture loosen slightly, my face softening as it forms an uncontained smile. Dunet has been interested in cooking for some time. With me being gone for large portions of each day, cooking must have been one of the many things to keep her preoccupied. I always felt a pleasant warmth towards Chef Feln, who has taken Dunet in like one of his very own professional cooks, admittedly with several benefits. My lips crinkle up at the thought. He has done more for her than I could have asked, especially since I would not have expected it. Her beautiful spark is hard not to let in. It makes me feel such comfort to know that the staff embraces and looks after her in my absence. I just wish they did not have to.

I meet his eyes meaningfully. "Thank you for your time, Chef Feln, and for taking care of my sister."

"We enjoy having her here," Chef Feln replies. "She is a genuine delight, and I know we will always welcome her."

"I am glad to hear it." I drop the conversation, trying to be respectful of his time. "I know you must have much to attend to. You are dismissed, Chef Feln."

He bows once more before turning back to his duties with a quick step.

I turn on my heel after he departs, instinctively transitioning into the long stride I have grown accustomed to as I walk out the kitchens and past the prestigious dining area and audience hall, back down the side corridor bordering the back side of the entry hall. I ascend the twisting staircase up to the wing of the lord, which houses my father and my family.

My eyes gloss over the smooth stonework and the evenly lit candles in the clefts of the stairwell. I climb as if there is a push at my back. Then I exit into a low, homely, regal hall, which is carpeted in crimson red with a low, arched ceiling, and the pale golds of evenly-spaced chandeliers and candle holders, giving the expanse a soft, warm look, like that from a living room fireplace stretched out into a corridor. Azure blue and forest green tapestries hang neatly, with beautifully hand-painted vistas, framing every few feet along the wall. Mother has certainly always loved adorning our home with paintings, something my father adopted when they married. He thought her tastes charming, and I cannot say I disagree, for it does bring a warmth to the place.

I make my first stop for today, as exhaustion begins to register in my mind. I feel a thrill, though, to see my father.

I turn into his office. Lord Fenor Ren Cordre is a noble-looking, refined man, with green-hazel eyes looking out from a kind face, that hides a hint of amusement, the creases of his workload show in small wrinkles overshadowed by the dimples of his unfaltering optimism and commitment, a short, neatly-trimmed beard, smooth, carefully-set jawline, and medium-length sandy hair over his burgundy-red suit, complete with gold buttons and sky-blue trim. His bearing, both steadying regal and lax, always brought an air of peace and comfort to me, dispelling much of my own tightness.

His office stands in plain grandness—an oval room with a tall ceiling and the curve of shelving on the back side. A huge antique-looking desk sits in the center, set neatly with stacks of paperwork for the city's functions. The room is otherwise sparse, besides a map of the continent, Ziluth, two crossed swords and the emblem of Claralis on an azure blue and forest green shield, a framed declaration of the city's founding and my father's title. There's another painting my father and mother received for their wedding. A detailed sketch of our family sits close to his workspace. I draw my attention to a few trinkets Dunet must have given him next to it, my own letter requesting admittance to Claralis' armies resting next to that. He is a sentimental man and always supportive of both my sister and me. He gave me my first practice sword, which I still house in my room. I feel quite comfortable both asking him for advice and relieving our joint stress together. That is always something we can laugh about.

"Father." I stand before his desk in a loose formality.

I almost chuckle. As my sister observed, he is surrounded by what seems like an endless stack of paperwork.

"Liela." His shoulders relax, and his mouth takes on a crisp, kindly smile, as he looks up from his work. His eyes are always accompanied by tired circles, but there's a light and charm to them that exhaustion never overshadows.

"My report from today." I bring out a folder, yet another document to add to Father's large workload. "Nothing of incidence, so my report is rather sparse." My lips quirk up at the corners. Fortunately for you, Father, I think. Of course, this is a copy of the report I had presented to the top military commander of the city, Commander Wheln. He has taken a liking to me, though I feel it is a bit too early to get my hopes up about anything, even if they rise nevertheless. I set my report on my father's desk with a flourish.

"Thank you, Liela." He takes it, shoulders relaxed, even if I can feel his slight frown as he looks down at it. "Did you enjoy yourself?" His voice is smooth and conversational.

"I did. The soldiers are in good morale these days. Almost too good." I settle with a slight grin.

"I hope not," he says with casual irony. "You're becoming quite the popular general." Father's voice lifts as he leans forward slightly. "I hear that Commander Wheln is considering you as his replacement."

"He thinks too highly of me." I try not to let my satisfaction show, maintaining my poise. I know I still have a long way to go. Still, I feel a small spark of pride in my chest.

"I think not." His hand brushes at the air. "Anyway, Liela, I'm proud of you. You have proven much more capable than me."

"All because of you, Father." I smile inwardly at the compliment. I see a mutual admiration and respect radiating in his eyes—the same that I hold for him.

"That aside, your presence has been requested by Lord Darnor Veln. He came this morning. I told him you were out."

I raise an eyebrow.

"He is quite fond of you, but I figured you may not want to see him."

I look gratefully at my father, even if Darnor's call chips at my mind. My lips purse.

I would much rather see Driena or Myllia right now … My mind flits to the courtyard I share with Myllia just briefly, before I bring my attention back to Darnor.

While he must realize I have no time for him, I have to admit: Darnor's company is welcome, even if it is increasingly agitating as of late. As annoying as it is, I trust that it will pass.

I change the subject after a short pause, refusing to let myself dwell on it too much. Father does not question it. "I heard mother was off today."

"She left this morning to settle a small matter in one of the villages to the east. She seemed to think she would be back by the evening."

I nod as my mind hazes over, my fingers twitching ever-so-slightly at my sides, as I refuse the tempting urge to bite my lip. I feel somewhat conflicted whenever she comes up, but I don't think I have a right to hold anything against her. "I trust that the visit goes well. If she gets back before this evening, my sister and I have something planned for this evening's meal." I let my voice rise back out of that dark veil I don't like to acknowledge.

Father perks up with a swivel of his brow and a sudden straightening of his back. "You two best get on with it, then. Dunet is probably bouncing off the walls in anticipation." Father then makes an exaggerated effort to get on with his work.

"That is putting it lightly." I join him, laughing without much reservation.

My father gives me a charming wink. "With that thought in my head, I think this paperwork will all be gone by the time you call me."

I dash a wink back, before descending into a dramatic bow and heading out of the room. I find myself grinning at father's antics. I always treasured our relationship and I looked up to him. I wish I could say the same for my mother, but I am happy enough to have Father by my side as I work towards becoming commander. I know we would work well together, as long as he holds onto his title. He is almost a mirror image of myself, in so many ways.

I close the cool oaken door to Father's office, stepping back into the hallway.

But when he gives that title up ...

I stiffen, my mind taut at the notion.

It is either me or her who take up Command of Claralis. I close my eyes. I am determined for it to be me. I open them again with burning resolve. I promised I would take the army for myself, and to protect Dunet—the thing I hold so desperately dear. I will take the army too—that I will do solely for my sister. I will not let that weight crush me. My heart lightens, because I know that I can and will take anything from her. She will always have the carefree life she deserves, and I will shield her from that burden with everything that I can offer her. Beyond my training as a knight, that is why I strive to excel in my studies as well.

I make a short stop at my room, just down the hall from my father's office. It is a rather sparse room, but still fit for a lord's daughter—large and cavernous, but neat and welcoming, a large bed in the center draped in simple white sheets, a cool blue rug around the bed, and a balcony opening to a view of the serene and imposing Kalltarris Mountains. I was never one for adorning my room. My real home is in my family and my city. My room is a temporary reprieve that I can let myself simply breathe in when I need to. I can fill my room with my thoughts, more than I can my possessions.

I unbuckle my sword belt and set it against my bed, taking off a few pieces of armor to look a bit more ceremonious. I can wash and change later, but for now, Dunet is my priority.

I take another glance at my room, before stepping out again.

Time to join my sister. Hopefully, the kitchen is still intact, I think to myself with a smile.

I turn near the end of the hallway into the living area to the right—cavernous, but still very homely. There's a sofa along the opposite edge and a fireplace in the center of the room. On the wall to the left lies a glass-paneled floor-to-ceiling window overlooking the glimmering lights in the sprawl of the city, and the snow blanketing the peaks of the Kalltarris Mountains cresting behind it in silence. The sun rapidly falls from brisk afternoon into hazy twilight.

I move over to the window, pausing for a moment, letting a calm silence sink over me.

Mine.

This is my city that I will protect.

I will always strive to be who my people need.

I place my hand against the pane.

A moment later, I shake myself out of my reverie. The most important light to protect is behind me.

I turn, passing the dining room through a low arch on the window side of the room. I move to the other side, to the kitchen, which is situated through a second arch, well-lit. Another window and an arch connect it directly to the dining room, and several candles light it aglow from across an elevated counter. The counters on two sides surround a central cutting table, and rest below an assortment of cabinets with fine silverware, mined from the nearby Kalltarris Mountains and fashioned as another wedding gift to my parents from a family friend.

I spot Dunet, who is looking intent in her bustle around the kitchen. I move to join her. As expected, she is brimming with energy, and I find my own energy lifting too.

"Liela, look at what I found!" Hurriedly, she runs over, a cookbook in her arms. She offers it to me, pointing to a certain recipe—carrot soup. My sister just loves carrots and I find myself unsurprised, my heart jubilantly soaring to join her in her wondrous frenzy.

"I am sure mother and father would love that!" I say. "Now, let us get to work. I bet Father is nearly done with his paperwork!"

I find myself almost as light as she is. Part of me wants to impress our father too, though I nearly choke thinking up his possible reactions.

Dunet bursts from her spot, excitedly running to the cupboards and cooling boxes to gather ingredients. With half of them already buried in her arms, she furiously hops to reach an elusive cabinet. I laugh at her efforts, before moving to help her.

With ingredients nearly drowning her, she moves to the counter, almost tripping over her feet as she deposits them on its surface.

I stop her hand as she reaches for a knife, my heart locking up for a moment, but I reign in that panic with a steadying breath. "I shall do the cutting, Dunet. You're not quite ready for that," I say as gently as I can, pressing my hand over the top of hers for emphasis. Her expression turns glum, and I give her a prodding smile. "How about you peel and wash the vegetables, and get the pot ready?"

She beams and hurries to her duties.

I look over at her, feeling tender at the sight of her joyousness. Sometimes I wonder if I hold her back too much, but there are many things which I do feel the need to do for her right now.

I turn back to the vegetables, holding onto that tender feeling. Cooking is practical, but something I never personally enjoyed. I am glad to have it at home, as it is another thing I can share with my sister.

~

27

Dunet looks down sunnily at the contents of the soup as I move it off the flame to cool, craning her neck over the lid to see.

"It looks so tasty!" she squeals. "I want mom and dad to try it!"

"It does look amazing! Go tell father that it's ready," I say, a gentle smile playing over my lips.

Dunet runs off, her bare feet pattering excitedly over the small stone tiles of the kitchen. I pause for a moment, before following, just waiting to hear her exclamation to father.

I hear Dunet's thrilled rush from down the hall. "We made something for you, Dad!"

I enter shortly after with a little more grace, and I see Dunet tugging on Father's sleeve.

He looks down, patting her head. "I will be there in just a moment." His voice sounds like a pleasant narrative from a book.

Dunet frowns.

He gives a drawn-out pause for emphasis. "But, if you insist, my paperwork can wait." He gets up, patting Dunet's head, then stretches out his limbs with an exaggerated groan. He looks down again, beaming with assurance. "Well, let me see what you created tonight!"

Dunet tugs on his wrist and leads him to the kitchen, my father following with a spring in his step. I cover my mouth in a laugh as they pass, and my father grins good-naturedly.

"It looks wonderful," Father exclaims as he takes his seat in a casual sweep, looking pleasantly at the soup sitting in the serving bowl.

Dunet beams at the compliment, even as her eyes flicker ever-so-slightly, one foot lightly tapping against the other.

"I just need to taste it. Before I do, I believe your mother should be arriving shortly." He looks meaningfully towards the hallway.

"You should wait for her, Father, while we finish preparations for the two of you."

"Perfect!" He sinks back against the chair, giving Dunet a soft, cradling look after the appraisal of her cooking.

I steer Dunet into the kitchen, placing my palm over her back. Then I reach down to hold her hand. She starts skipping to the kitchen, and I feel a spring in my step as well.

I reach into the cupboards for bowls and Dunet grabs the silverware—beautifully etched with a dandelion over each handle.

Not many moments later, I hear our mother's collected, firm voice with an underlying sweetness mingling with Father's, from the dining room.

Dunet bounds out of the room, and I try to grasp at her, to no avail. "Careful, Dunet!" I insist, my stomach dropping as her hands wrap loosely around the silverware.

"Mommy!" she cries, flinging her arms around her.

Mother picks Dunet up, bringing her face close to her own in a warm coddle. "I have missed you today, Dunet. I hear you made us soup!"

"We did!" Dunet curls her toes out beneath her as her face flushes. I think her feet must be freezing, but she hardly ever wears shoes, just simple fluttering dresses of whites and light blues and greens, sometimes daffodil yellow; occasionally it's ruffles and maybe a bracelet, but she nearly always insists on something simple.

Mother pauses, unwrapping her arms from Dunet and setting her lightly on the ground. She reaches experimentally into the pockets of her knee-length, light-plum travel coat. "I brought something home for you from my visit." She pulls out a piece of savory-looking rosemary bread.

Dunet takes it with relish, hopping as her small hands reach forward. I can see her mind twirling. "We can eat this with the soup!"

Mother smiles calmly at Dunet, her eyes shaded pleasantly. "That would be a terrific idea!" She then raises her eyes to me, and they dull slightly, her face dropping to a stonier formality, even if that laurel smile lingers at her lips.

"Mother." I nod, an acknowledgement but nothing more, as I feel the unsteady twinge of my heart. Neither of us closes that distance anymore. I accepted that we may never be close again, even if I initially felt a gaping divide that nearly suffocated me at the time. That pain is still there, it has just gotten easier to hide.

Her smile fades slightly, but she holds onto it—something barely noticeable. But I do notice it, as it tugs at my chest with a cold weight. "It's good to see you too, Liela," but it sounds much too deflated.

I never saw any tenderness at my choices, just that glazed mist across her eyes. Maybe she was just afraid of the risk and started distancing herself from me, or maybe it was something else, the possibility of which still clouds my mind. I was always closer to Father, as Dunet is closer to Mother. Those chains and yearning chasms only seem to grow stronger and fade as we age. I wish it all never happened. I parse my lips ever-so-slightly, and force a short exhale, trying to fade it from my mind. I can lament about it, but it will not do me any good. I am worth enough that I will not let myself dwell on it.

I find it sad, really, a pit in my heart that I want to desperately claw at, but I think it's best to let go. I was still too young to really understand what was going on at the time. I admit that I am ... uncomfortable at how to approach fixing our relationship. It's far easier to leave it as it is now, just a distant memory.

I am shaken out of my thoughts at the bittersweet image of her and my sister. "That would be a perfect use for it!" Mother clasps her hands together, her voice blossoming. "Come, you must have been waiting for a great deal of time. Let us eat; I want to try your creation!"

"And Liela's," Dunet interjects, that pure insistence still in her eyes, not a single shadow.

"Yes, and Liela's." Her eyes retreat just enough to stab me.

Mother stands, then draws herself into her chair gracefully. She is an elegant woman—gorgeous and refined, her long, brunette hair plaited over her back, matching perfectly with her coat. Her face is an etched softness over stern cheekbones, mouth a commanding line under full lips, rosy cheeks, and light, crystalline blue eyes and full lashes that manage to capture the attention of everyone in a room.

Dunet moves to sit on her lap and mother resigns herself to it with a treasuring smile.

I move back to the kitchen, where I finish ladling the soup into bowls. Reentering the dining room, my movements are as practiced and calm as ever.

I have always been a collected person—calm and never irritated. I find it easy to get along with people, though I can be assertive when I need to be. It's only difficult around my mother, but I do pride myself in that fact.

I sit down in my chair, looking rather dignified and knightly, but not imposing. I am still quite present with my family, no matter how I portray myself.

Father shares a mischievous look with me from across the table, as he receives his food and then gives his customary wink. In this setting, that means he is thanking me and adding some humor to his hunger. I wink back at him, even if I find myself nearly rolling my eyes at his antics.

Father, as usual, abandons much of his formality at the dinner table, even if he lets the bare traces remain. He dips his spoon into the soup with a swift flurry, working in his praise after several bites. "This is very good soup. You two did an excellent job!"

Mother then takes an elegant spoonful. "Delicious ... That was thoughtful of you." She gives Dunet a short peck on the cheek.

Dunet's dimples deepen, before she tucks her head at the attention, tapping her pointer fingers together as she looks between them. I give a knowing look at Father, then continue with my meal.

"How was your visit today, Mother?" I bring up the reason for her absence, sitting back with a loosening of my shoulders, even as my ears prick, and I lean forward just a little.

Mother waves her hand with a flitting grace. "Trivial for the most part. There were some slight concerns with the supply lines as of late. I had to reassure them that I would address the issue once I got back. Otherwise, the village is doing quite well."

I nod. I consider broaching the topic now, but decide to do it again later, if it should still seem pertinent.

As the wife to the lord of Claralis, mother had stepped into her own position. I do admire her for taking up a place of importance alongside father, much more than I would like to admit. She acts as a voice to Claralis, overseeing matters of relations. I could consider her position almost as important as my father's.

"And how was your day, Dunet?" Mother loosens her arms as Dunet cranes her neck back at her.

Dunet looks back with a glint in her eyes, a bite halfway to her mouth. "It was boring! Everyone was so busy today!" She pouts, her cheeks puffed. "Until Liela got home!" She looks at me with a love that cushions my heartstrings.

Mother casts a glance at me with a genuine gratitude, even if there are still undertones of a shadow to it.

"Liela said she would take me riding sometime too!" Dunet adds, her gaze turning swiftly to me.

"Did she?" Mother raises her eyes to me.

I take a short, considerate pause. "As soon as I find the time for it, that is. In fact, Father and I have a horse just for you." I pitch my voice a little higher, in indication for Dunet. "We were going to let you help raise her."

Dunet's face is radiant, as she bounces slightly on mother's lap, her eyes flecked with sunshine.

"It should give you someone else to play with," Father adds, twirling his spoon animatedly. "After all, my paperwork really is endless." He shows a bit of exaggerated dejection at that last part, slumping back into his seat.

I snort under my breath, then add, "Just think of Dunet riding in a few weeks."

Father laughs heartily, giving Dunet an adoring look. "Well, I cannot say I will not be waiting for that day. Dunet, I know you will do excellently!"

Dunet giggles at the compliment. "When can I see her?"

"Hm." Father rests his chin over his fist and looks at me contemplatively. "I think you may just get off early tomorrow. Is that so, Liela?"

"I believe so. My duties are limited tomorrow, unless anything pressing occurs." I rest my hand on the table, tapping my pointer finger lightly against the sanded wood, before turning away from Father to Dunet. "I believe I could let you see her tomorrow, once I finish with all my duties."

Dunet's smile swells. "Yay!"

My mother places her hands over hers slightly to calm her.

"I know she will love you, Dunet." My sister could use another friend and I do really look forward to now being able to ride with her. I have taken her on some trips saddled with her, but this is a little bit different. I wonder if that is a bad thing. It does bring me a sense of security to have her strapped to me, but this could be something different—something fun and new that we can share. I shake my head. It will be perfect, and I smile back at her, this time with dimples of my own.

Dunet breaks our gaze first, to look back at Mother. I make an effort to dismiss the abrupt tension that nabs at me. It is just a passing thing, and I will have several hours tomorrow to spend with her, I reason with myself.

Mother combs her fingers through Dunet's hair in a calming motion. "Maybe when you know how to ride, we can take you on a picnic someplace?"

I curl my hands under the table. Snap out of it, Liela! It bothers me when I am irritated. I should know better. I close my eyes for a moment, soothed again by Dunet's voice. There's nothing wrong with what Mother said and I let out a tense sigh. The smile comes back to my face a moment later.

"Oooo!" she squeals. "Can we go now?" Her concentration falls back on me.

"Tomorrow," I remind her, with a patient tone.

Her face falls for a moment, but she then turns back to her food with a renewed appetite.

I take another spoonful of mine. My mind turns to thinking about tonight—just a short meeting, a night to rest, and then I can pick up Dunet in the morning. There is really not much to go over.

"Anyway, Fenor," Mother's voice comes out neatly, "I will be off again tomorrow, to check on the villages around Lyrell. It has me slightly worried and I wanted to inquire more about the incident with the supply lines. I have a few acquaintances to meet with tonight and I wanted to speak to you about it."

Father nods to her with a creased brow. "Of course, Fern." Fern is mother's first name—Fern Mella Cordre.

I almost tell Mother to notify me of any leads, before sitting back and reminding myself that the information will likely get to me if it becomes important. I remain silent.

Mother knows what she is doing, and I know that I am not commander yet. I will not be getting ahead of myself now. I am not that arrogant, to assume what information Mother and Father should share with me when it comes to their city. It's nothing personal, even if I cannot help wanting to know.

Mother picks up her napkin, dusting it against her mouth, then she rises out of her chair, placing Dunet back on her seat. "I think I had better be going. I will be in my room preparing, Fenor, and I expect to be back in no less than two hours."

Father takes her hand and kisses it. "Take care."

"Of course, Fenor," she says gently.

Dunet circles the table to me, waving quickly to our mother. I slip out of my chair, kneeling in front of her. "Are you ready for bed, Dunet?"

"Mhmmm!" She nods, sounding it out, before she gives an exaggerated yawn.

"Okay, then." I lead her to her room. She pulls me in the other direction, towards mine, and I know instinctively what she wants. I let her lead me there.

I pull open the door and she rushes over, throwing the covers off. Then she settles down, eyeing me as she tugs the covers over her chin.

I climb into bed beside her. "All right, Dunet ..."

She stares at me with eager, orb-like sapphire eyes.

I begin in a lull. "There was a girl who met a horse one day. That was all the girl had ever asked for. She was sweet and loving and the girl brought her carrots every day."

Dunet giggles, covering her mouth with the blankets.

"One day, the girl climbed atop her and whispered in the horse's ear to take her as far as she possibly could, to the ends of the Earth, if possible. The horse obliged, taking the girl as fast as she could over the ground, until they were soaring like the wind!" My voice soars. "The girl loved it. She loved the feel of the wind in her hair, the smell of grass and flowers and woods, the burbling of silent brooks in the meadows, and the sky stretching out before her. The girl reached both her hands out, grasping at the clouds, giggling and giggling until her voice was hoarse. She clung to the horse's neck with tiny hands, until they were finally there, and the girl laughed at the beautiful golden sunset over the lapping waters of the sea. They stared in awe for what seemed to the girl to be years, until the horse told the girl it was time to go home. The girl insisted the horse was her home and that she loved her. She was happy, but pleaded with the girl that she had to take her home; there were people who missed her and things she had to do. The girl reluctantly complied, and they rode back. The girl was tucked into her warm bed, dreaming of the next day. The horse was there again, day-after-day, and the girl was as happy as a spring flower in bloom.

"Do you not want to stay here, the horse asked one day, to which the girl shook her head, replying that she wanted to go on more adventures, forever and ever! And the horse couldn't stop herself, for she loved the girl and the girl loved her. The girl ran, until she ran alone. Looking behind her, she realized that she was no longer riding with her friend, for she ran too fast and too far, until she was lost ...

"She did not know what to do, so she pretended and pretended. She would forever run and ride and skip, even when her own doubt would tie her down. But ... she knew she was free ... that she had to be ... because she was still running ..."

I look down to find Dunet asleep, and I bend down, giving her a cradling kiss. "Goodnight, Dunet."

Her eyes flutter like wings, and she asks, "What happened to the girl?"

I reply with a brush of stardust. "She lived happily-ever after."

"I'm ... glad ..." she murmurs, her eyes trailing as she snoozes into my shoulder.

"The girl had a happily ever after," I whisper to myself in a haze, as I press my head back against the pillow and let my own sleep come to me. It brings a tender smile to my face as my mind settles, knowing that she did not hear the end. But maybe it's a good ending after all. Because...she still ran, a shining flower looking ever to a magical sunset.

~ Memory ~

Passage of Dreams

Dunet

I rub at my eyes, scrunching them shut, but I cannot go back to sleep. I stare up at the painted stars on my ceiling, rolling over and grasping at my fluffy, stuffed bunny—Ceilia, who brings a warm tingling to my mind, letting my breath settle. But I still cannot sleep. My mind roils, feeling the creeping shadows. I roll over, slipping from my bed in a clumsy effort and onto the cottony-blue rug, in the shred of moonlight from my curtain.

I quietly tiptoe down the hall, feeling magical, like a little princess in my silk-white nightgown. A small chill passes up my spine and I clutch guardedly against Ceilia in my arms.

I start bounding a little and then jump at a small noise, shrieking suddenly and slowing down again to a pad.

Liela would calm me; she always does.

I tiptoe to her door, pushing it open a crack and peeking in.

I can see the sheets ruffle, as if she senses me in the doorway. She calls to me in a comforting voice. "Dunet, you should be in bed by now." Her soft olive eyes beckon me. The dark browns of her hair fall behind her ears, and her hands are placed patiently over the bedsheets.

"I want you to tell me stories," I let loose in a hurried voice, barely above a whisper.

"All right, Dunet." She calls to me with open arms. "Come here." She smiles warmly, as if she expected this. "Just one and then I will send you off to bed." My face lights up and I move towards her bed, my nightgown swishing in ripples through the moonlight.

I like Liela's room. It feels cradling and kind and close. It feels like a fairytale adventure sparking to life in the silver moonlight.

She pulls the covers off one side, making room for me. I climb in, snuggling up next to her.

"Which one would you like to hear, or should I tell you a new one?" she asks with a soft, slow cadence, as she brushes my hair, her head resting close to mine.

I think for a minute. "I want to hear a new one!"

Liela pauses for a moment, her brow creasing, before her face turns to softness once more. Her voice always seems to change when she reads a story, flowing softly like a stream, yet still composed and direct in her tone.

"There was a maiden once." Her voice sounds dream-like. "Her name was Genaia—beautiful and beloved by her people, but also strong and fierce, a warrior-queen. She loved her sister Veir more than anyone else and would do anything for her. But, one day, her sister fell ill. To save her, Genaia had to travel seemingly endlessly to find something, anything that could save her."

I feel a pressing tingle creep at my mind. My breath picks up as I wonder what Genaia would do. "I know she can do it," I whisper.

Liela gives me a comforting smile and continues. "She heard a rumor of a remedy to the north, so she headed out with the sunrise. The remedy was the Xephir Flower, said to have the ability to cure all ailments. This flower was guarded by a legendary dragon, fierce as burning flame. It was a flower clearer than the clearest sky, housed on the highest peak in the world, far away from any person."

I gasp as my heart leaps.

"Genaia climbed the mountain and slew the dragon. She was able to save Veir, on the brink of death. She burst into tears of relief and joy upon her recovery and their reunion in good health, for Veir was frightened for her sister too.

"Genaia became a leader of her people thereafter, with her sister ever in her thoughts and supporting her at her side. She was a warrior queen nevertheless, and the two were torn apart by an unforeseen war, prompting Genaia to defend her people and her dearest sister. Veir wished with her entire heart for her sister's safety in battle, even if, with each day, came a pang of longing for her far-off sister. And with dreaded news, Veir learned of Genaia's fall in battle. She was torn apart by grief and despair at the loss of her sister. Genaia was forever in her thoughts, but she learned to accept that her sister would want her to be happy and live a long, prosperous life. While she missed her sister dearly, she promised herself she would live a fulfilled life, holding dear her sister's sacrifice. That bond was never broken, remaining in the stars and in Veir's heart." Liela trails off like the fading tail of light on a shooting star.

I remain silent, the story jabbing at my mind, unable to grasp it, as if the meaning can only be reached through a thick veil.

"Maybe that wasn't the happiest ending," Liela says soothingly. "I find it bittersweet. Perhaps I should tell you a different story."

"I wish Genaia had not died ..." I murmur. "Why did Genaia leave for war?"

"To protect her sister," Liela tells me softly, her warm eyes aglow.

"But could she not have protected her some other way?"

Liela looks at me for a moment with a drifting expression, before answering. "Perhaps, but that was all she knew."

"I want to hear another," I reply a little weakly.

Liela smiles, shifting her gaze past the open curtains. "There exists a country, Florrell—an idyllic country of green grasses flowing like waves in an ocean and beautiful waterfalls falling into shallow streams winding through patches of emerald forest, into the sparkling of crystal-clear lakes. All of it, in a peaceful isolation surrounded by the calm of the ocean. It is a country of music and laughter and dancing—of the harp and flute, violin and viola and piano ... rolling softly on a bed of dream-like complacency ..."

I drift slowly into sleep at her pleasant voice, the fairytale image alight in my imagination, until my dreams transport me to that magical place, with Liela by my side ...

~ Memory ~

To Protect a Flower

Liela

I walk purposefully into Father's office, even with my still small frame, my chin held exaggeratedly high as I crane up at his office.

I stand a little taller, resting my arms over my father's desk, and stare over my arms as he works.

I can see the tap of a smile creep over his features as he feigns ignoring me, reading over the contents of several lengthy papers and scribbling his name at the bottom in a breezy rush.

He sets his quill down, reaching over to ruffle my hair. Then meets my unflinchingly bright gaze. "It's late, Liela. Go see Dunet," he offers to me kindly, more a suggestion than an order.

"I like working with you."

"You can work with me all you want when you're older," he settles with a small assurance, "but there are more important things right now."

My chest eases somewhat, but I push myself forward again, failing to let up, to which my father chuckles. "What did you just sign?" I ask.

"Do you really want to know?" He brings his hands together, casually posing them on the desk.

I rest my chin onto my arms, pushing further forward, twisting my toe in my shoe on the carpet out behind me.

"It's a funding agreement from the capital, Siltheus— a five percent subsidy to fortifications. I had put in a request for additional funding for residential services." His forehead creases. "But it looks like I will not be getting it. You don't have to worry, though." He smiles at me delicately.

I latch onto his words. "I want you to enroll me in the military!" I blurt a bit too fast. I want to come off serious and sure, for Father. "You said I can work by your side." I slow down, trying to sound clearer. "I want to protect Dunet."

"You're a stubborn girl. Just two more years to think about it and then you can enroll." His smile is fond, but still set firmly in place. "If that is still what you want, then you can have my full approval."

I feel a steady dissipation in my chest that I try not to show, and I force myself to let up some, shifting my weight back again. "I think you might be tired, Father." I prickle him lightly. "You should come see Dunet with me."

"Of course, Liela. As impatient as my attendants may be for a signature, I will endure their wrath for my daughters!" He gives a resounding chuckle.

I snort, and burst into laughter.

"Though, fortunately, they don't mind enough," he adds.

Father rises, cringing slightly from the hours of work he spent sitting down. "Though if you work with me at all, you may regret getting old. I think it's infectious."

"Less than Dunet's youth," I say with a rallying smile.

"Good point. With that, I think I do need an extended break with my exceptional daughters." He moves out from behind the desk with a flourish. I wait for him to come closer, before falling into step beside him in growing delight.

A moment later, with a bit of a falling feeling, I ask, "But what about your work?"

His eyes find me and comfort me like a blanket. "It can wait, for now. You know that you, Dunet, and your mother are the most important things to me? Well, there are days when I really might not have the time, so I want to make the time now."

I cling to his side, feeling weightless at his attention, even if I wonder if I was being rude, but he does not seem too distracted. I follow him, my heart soaring even further to the stars. I wonder if I can really have my wish to protect Dunet and walk behind my father as a leader to my people ...

A Never-Ending Softness

Liela

My eyes are far too intent, as I have no duties to attend to right now. I try to ignore the constant press on my conscience. All I must do is remind myself that I get to spend this time with Dunet and that is all I need to put my heart at ease.

Because Dunet is why I work so hard. She always has been.

A part of me wonders if I will get to see Myllia today too, though I quickly brush the thought aside. Dunet comes first, before anything. Though Myllia's cornflower eyes and curls flash in my mind for a second longer, before my attention turns to my sister once more.

I make my way over to the dining room, pausing on my way under the arch to the living room. I try to decide whether or not to wake her up, but I know her better. She is probably up and about, eager for the day ahead.

The sun strikes through the high windows of the living room in waves, coloring the space in a pleasant haze. This morning is a peaceful respite from my packed schedule. I find Father in a chair by the corner, humming to himself quietly as he glosses over a book.

He looks up at me, eyes welcoming. "Up early?"

"Hardly. It is a little late for my liking. I am surprised to find you up, Father."

He lowers the book. "Dunet is in the kitchen. I thought I would brush up on my reading while she is at it. I find that I am rather lacking in that regard." He keeps his face utterly straight.

"Clearly." I raise my eyebrows, also keeping an unbearably straight face and stifling my laugh. "Good morning, Father."

"Good morning. Call me when it's ready, if you could?"

"I will do just that," I say with a jostling grin, stepping past his chair and moving the few remaining steps to the kitchen.

I find Dunet prancing around, putting together four small servings of buttered toast and strawberries and a healthy serving of oats with a side of fresh market eggs and steamed spinach.

She turns to me with a spin. "Good morning, Liela!" Then she casts her eyes away, foot dragging with a muted squelch over the floorboards, strawberry juice smeared across her hands and mouth.

"Good morning, Dunet," I say calmly.

She gives a hiccup followed by a giggle, covering her mouth, and eyeing me guiltily.

I cannot help it, and break into a frenzied laugh. After I catch my breath, I cross the room to join her. "Can I help you with anything Dunet?"

She looks down at the plate in her hand with an unbreaking, tiny intensity, giving her head a drifting shake to the side.

"How about I help you carry it out?" I move to the counter, scooping up two dishes and heading to the entrance.

She steps in next to me, looking at me with clear, light eyes.

Father waits for us, leaning back a bit too lazily for a lord. I honestly cannot figure out how he manages to keep a relaxed attitude and still be seen as competent. Still, that is my father as I know him, and this city would hardly be the same without him.

Dunet brings the plate forward.

"Why thank you, Dunet!" he praises as he takes it in a gentle reverie.

Dunet beams, even as her gaze flits downwards. "You're welcome!" She raises her head in a show of confidence, before her eyes turn away again.

Father waves his fork shrewdly. "And there's no need to be modest. You did an astounding job Dunet!"

Dunet shuffles her feet, but her eyes return again to look upon our father.

"Are you coming to the table, Father?"

"I certainly would, but this view is quite ..." He purses his lips in thought, glancing at the window. "Quaint."

"Well, it's settled then."

Dunet leaps onto a chair near Father's and rests her chin against the armrest, squinting at the light from outside.

"Dunet, you should not do that; it will damage your eyes!" I comment hastily.

She lifts her head, staring back at me with bulbous eyes, before she casts them down, her gaze deflated. "Sorry, Sister."

"Dunet, it's okay," I assure her warmly. "There's no need for that."

"Yes." She nods meekly.

I move to sit, straight-backed, but with my legs crossed gracefully in front of me. Taking a bite from my toast, I grin. "I agree with Father. You did a fine job, Dunet."

She bounces again. "I got it all from Chef Feln this morning! But ..." She frowns. "He said the strawberries would not be good for much longer."

"That is very disappointing," I say, frowning as well. "You will have to eat a lot!"

She giggles again, her eyes moving hungrily to the strawberries.

After a moment, I ask her the question I have been longing to ask: "Are you ready to ride with me today, Dunet?"

"I am! I am so excited!" She bounces in her seat, her words hardly comprehensible. "I want to meet her!"

She starts to stand, and I finish my food in a hurry, before picking up father's dishes and Dunet's.

"You girls have fun for me." Father dashes a warm, lax grin.

"We will, Father!" I add crisply, "I know Dunet will bring you back a present." I move to the sink to wash the dishes.

"Should I help you with those?" I hear him call after me.

"No need this morning," I remark at the few dishes we have.

"I suppose I can stay here then." I hear him say from the room over.

I do them quickly and then move back up to meet Dunet who bounds out to me and then follows in my footsteps. Father waves at me with a gloss of his hand and I wave back.

I descend the steps as Dunet pulls ahead of me, skipping every other step.

I must resist the urge to pull her back and tell her to be careful.

We move through the hall, Dunet so intent on riding that she nearly bumps into the bustling castle staff, lords, soldiers, and servants. I reach to pull her back as she nearly collides with a nice-looking servant girl. "Watch your step, Dunet!" I caution, then add courteously to the servant girl, "We are very sorry."

She nods absently, then throws a short smile down at Dunet. "It is perfectly alright." And then she looks back up to me with a "Thank you" and a short bow, her eyes wide.

Dunet looks to me guiltily and then falls back to my side, grabbing my hand as if to placate me.

The entry columns go past us, then the gaping bronze double-doors, and we are out into the fresh dawn air. Dunet trails me as we reach the stables, the wood and iron trimming a welcome sign. It rises out of the neatly cut grass of the grounds in a rectangular form, the roof cresting upward in a curved spiral.

I push open the pen doors, moving towards a horse that is becoming familiar to me by now—a smaller mare suited to Dunet's height.

Dunet rushes over to her, reaching for her mane, but she then looks back at me before her hand touches her. "Does she have a name?"

"Her name is Eriena," I say, after a short pause. "I picked her out with Father, between work."

Dunet turns back to the mare, a broad grin and a giggle forming on her lips. "Hi, Eriena! My name is Dunet! We are going to have so much fun together!" As if in acknowledgement, Eriena leans her head further into Dunet's hand and it brings a smile to my lips. I knew Dunet would like her, but it pulls gently at my heartstrings even more to see her reaction.

"Would you like to ride her, Dunet?" I push warmly.

"Can I?"

"Of course! I said I would take you riding with me when I found the time. I will go grab Vel."

I move back into the stable, letting Dunet have a few moments alone with Eriena. Vel is near the back, a fine mare with tawny hair and intelligent, caring eyes. I pat her head lightly, move to saddle her, and lead her out of the pen. As I come back out into the open air, I find Dunet feeding Eriena a carrot.

"Do you like it, Eriena?" Dunet asks.

Eriena nibbles at the carrot, her soft eyes on Dunet.

"I know you do!" Dunet reaches up to stroke Eriena's mane, looking adoringly at her new friend. She must hear the crunch of my boots a moment later, because she looks back at me.

"Are you ready to mount her?"

"Yes!" she says in a flurry. Eagerly, she tries climbing into the saddle, but her foot fumbles around the stirrup as she hops repeatedly, to no avail.

I move behind her, to which she laughs in glee, squirming in my grip as I place her in the saddle and make sure everything is secure. I walk back over to Vel, mounting with ease, and I trot up alongside Dunet.

She gives me a glittering smile, her dimples clear as the sun. I give her a smile back. "Are you ready?"

"Yes!" she nods, bouncing in the saddle and reigning in just enough to keep from toppling from her seat.

I lead Eriena out, pulling her on a rope tied to a ring attached to her bridle, so we can practice outside. I stop in the practice field, the castle reaching with familiarity at my back and the walls of the outer castle not far away over the green lawn. Dunet turns to me with a searching look.

I give her a coddling smile. "I will show you a few simple commands and then you can try Dunet." I demonstrate commands to go, stop, and turn and then swing out of the saddle, striding lightly over to Dunet. "Now, can you make her go?"

I can see the creases on her forehead at her inexperience.

"I will be right here, so that you don't fall."

Dunet clicks her heels in the stirrups, fumbling precariously, and braces herself forward in a squeal.

I reach my hand out quickly, before it rests calmly on Eriena's flank. "That was good. Try it again."

She tries it several more times. Eriena seems to understand Dunet's inexperience and remains patient and steady. She is a good girl, just like Dunet. I find myself thinking that they make a good match.

I let her practice a while longer. Dunet gradually grows less tense, even if she still clings to the reins with a tight grip. Every once in a while, I cast her an approving gaze and let her eyes, alight with a new wonder, set my heart ablaze.

At some point, I think she must be hungry. I trot up alongside her. "Are you ready for lunch, Dunet?" I ask in a soothing voice.

"No!" she fizzles. "I want to ride more!"

"And we can!" I pat Vel, then dismount in a fluid motion and cross the short distance to her, holding out my arms for her to jump into. "But another time. I promise you will have nearly all the time in the world."

She looks back down to Eriena and then bends forward to murmur in her ear, while putting her arms around her neck, "I will be back to see you Eriena, because you're my friend now. It was so exciting to ride with you today!"

Eriena gives an affectionate whinny, nuzzling Dunet and pawing the ground in response.

Dunet tentatively brings her leg over Eriena's side, her fingers trembling against the pommel as her eyes dart to me.

"I am right here," I say with an ever-present protectiveness for her.

She takes a small breath and then jumps, her arms spiraling and her eyes wild like a scared dove, but I catch her.

She twines her arms around me tightly, releasing a tense giggle.

My eyelids flutter shut in the warm sunbeams, and I feel an incandescent wetness at the corners of my eyes. "I am glad you like her," I whisper in her ear, feeling the little warmth of her cheek and the exuberance pulsing underneath. I pull her back from me, looking into her pure, sapphire eyes. "Now, time to get you home," I say, brushing back her buttery hair from her dimpled cheeks. "We need to fill that stomach of yours!" I pinch her cheek and she breaks down into a fit of giggles.

I set her down, grasping her little hand as I put Eriena and Vel back in their pens. We make our way back to the castle, the greens of the dewy grasses springing up from under our feet.

Dunet starts skipping up the azure blue carpet of the castle steps, under the rising glass of the ceiling. She sags on the steps up to our tower, glancing back at me. "Liela, I am tired." Her voice is now filled with drowsiness and her eyelids droop.

I pick her up and she rests her head on my shoulder. "Then, I will just have to carry you." I can feel her breath lighten as I cradle her in my arms. Before we reach the top, she is fast asleep.

A fuzzy feeling dapples in my chest as I smile, walking through the hallway and whispering to my sister in quiet comfort, as I make my way to her room.

I start singing softly to her, out of habit. Occasionally I would do that for her, instead of telling her a story—lullabies I sing just for her.

The softness of snow;

The worries of a dove;

A stream singing to you softly,

57

As you curl at its edge.

You are a girl who is loved,

In your cradle of clouds,

The sky sinks to embrace you;

Stars settle on your brow.

To sleep in peace until the morning,

When the birds wake you,

And the sun welcomes you,

Your toes curl around the softness of grass.

    I tuck her into her bed, pulling the covers snuggly up under her rosy cheeks, and I bend down to kiss her lightly on her forehead.

And as you wake,

I bend to kiss your forehead,

Telling you just how much I love you,

Your eyes forever wrapped in starlight.

Caroline Sophia Hamel

~ Memory ~

Repose to a Soft Touch

Liela

I twirl my practice sword, glancing conspiratorially at Father, a glint in my eye and in his ... then I rush him. I tend to be a bit more energetic and impulsive around him. I suppose he brings out my rebellious side.

Looking polished despite the situation, he hardly flinches, giving me a self-assured smile. He is a fine warrior, despite the focus on his studies and his political position. My blow meets his sword, as expected, and I quickly shift my footing, backing off and looking for a counterattack, my forehead wrinkled in concentration.

Father practices with me on occasion, between his work and my training and studies. He insists on it, and I gladly oblige. I am always glad for any time with him as father-and-daughter, whether that is time spent joking, training, sharing our sense of workload, or sometimes just talking, because I do usually feel comfortable enough to talk at least on some level with him. Despite his more relaxed and humorous nature, he is quite perceptive.

I feint a cut from underneath and then quickly pull the wooden blade back, shifting to a diagonal cut.

He parries, his own forehead lined with a deep crease and his grip sturdy.

I grit my teeth as Father stays on the defensive. It is a very effective strategy in forcing me to exhaust myself, but even so, given my practice, I know I can do better. I find my opening, stop the swing just before it hits, and draw back my sword, thus marking the end of the match.

Father chuckles, a light sweat on his brow. "I can see your training is going well."

My lips curl up in a satisfied grin and I toss the practice sword to the side, sinking back onto the grass. "I would hope so." I relax, grabbing my knees. The stonework of the castle casts down splattered shadows accompanied by shade from the swaying boughs of the trees in the courtyard and the lazy clouds drifting in the blue, early summer sky above. It's hotter than usual today, and I reach the back of my hand up to rub at my brow.

Father sits down next to me. "And what does Commander Wheln think of you?" I can see a knowing gleam in his eyes before I can even reply, but I have never liked bragging about my accomplishments, even when they made my chest soar in pride. I always keep those emotions to myself.

I shrug. "He seems happy with my progress, and that is all I can ask for."

"You know, Liela, maybe you could get some air outside your fellow soldiers and Dunet? Find someone you want, not because of how you're connected. Maybe someone special." He puts it out casually, hiding a pointed look from under his brows, though I have a very good indication of what he means. I find it hard to know whether I should find it humorous or annoying, and I lean to the former, feeling the tentative twinge of my lips, even if my mind retreats from the subject.

"I think I am quite fine with what I have. I have Driena by my side and the other soldiers." I clutch harder onto my knees, staring at the sky with a wisp of thought. "And I have Dunet. I know you have a point though. Besides, I am part of the ruling family, it would do me some good." My lips slow to concede. I sigh. "Please, don't mention a love interest yet. I know, Father, but it's not on my mind."

"Fair enough," he continues casually. My mind settles once again, the momentary stiffness leaving my shoulders. "I would tell Dunet the same, though. She has no one besides you, from what I can tell. You are a bad influence." He chuckles once more.

"And your joke isn't funny." I glare at him with a sharpness to my tongue. "I just want her happy. Besides that, I have plenty of people to lean on, Father. It is Dunet you should be worried about, with whatever you're pushing." I give an eye roll at that.

"Of course. What I was trying to say, is that sometimes you're too focused, Liela. It matters, but I think you could do with some rest."

I lay back in the grass, letting the projections of leaves play over my eyelids. I close them for a moment. I have what I need and want—everything that I do. It has never bothered me that I put my heart into everything, because that is what I want and who I am. "Thank you, Father. You know I will think about it."

"You have not done anything wrong; it was just a bit of advice. You may not need it. I think you're in a stable place, but it never hurts."

"Of course." I wave my hand, my eyes still closed in a reverie to the soft light.

"Dunet is getting the same talk, minus the romance aspect." Of course, I smile. She is only twelve. I am not even sure how I would or could handle something so monumental, and I think it best not to think about.

I feel rooted and easy in his advice and his thoughts, but I am also afraid that if I ever brought up Dunet's lack of friends, around her age, at least ... Well, I guess I worry that it may push her away. It is unreasonable and unfair, but part of me wants to keep her all to myself. Sometimes I feel as if I could be a better role model to her, in some regards.

I hear the shifting of Father's weight and sit up as he stands. "You should get some rest, Liela. I had better get on with my paperwork."

"Good luck, Father."

"I will do my very best!" he replies with a polished smile and a bow.

I curl my fingers in the grass, feeling an itch on my skin as well at Father's implied insistence on romance. I honestly don't know what I want with that. Besides, I feel awkward and uncomfortable outside my motivations and the circle of people I include as family or friends. If anything, I try to avoid it. I would rather not be viewed romantically, if I could help it—not that I am viewed as desirable by others, anyway. Not in my mind, at least.

I move my hand up, watching the shadows of branches play off my skin just a little longer.

But ... It makes me feel a bit off.

And yes, maybe I don't show it much, but a part of me was always a little self-conscious about interactions I wasn't familiar with. It is a trait I hide well; I am popular among my fellow soldiers, and well-liked. That leaves me with such a pleasant stirring in my heart. I have many strengths and I acknowledge them. I love them all back like a second family.

I pull myself up, grasping my knees and dusting at my grass-caked pants.

I listen to the birds for another moment, trying to figure out where to go, then make my way out the edge of the courtyard, under the ivy-covered arch, feeling the familiar tendrils at my fingertips. I circle through the maze-like courtyard gardens, letting the contemplative silence envelop me. I love these gardens, but I don't spend nearly enough time here. Some of them are quite old, originating from the formation of the city. My father's mother spent a great deal of time restoring and expanding the gardens, even brightening the city by creating more outside the castle walls—Andrea Cordre, my grandmother. I suppose I developed my reading and storytelling habits from her. She is old now and her memory is leaving her. I miss her bright smile. I have Dunet to recite more stories to now, though, and I think that she would be glad.

I pass under another shadow of an arch, the sunlight flitting once more through the tangled ivy and falling in glimmering shades on another courtyard, bright and welcoming, magical even. A fountain rests to the side of the entrance, gurgling calmly. The grasses curve into small inclines, mixed in with flowers of various shades of purple, yellow, white, and pink. A tree waves lazily, almost dream-like, its boughs cresting over the waters of a still pond, the barest of ripples from the summer breeze brushing its glimmering surface as it reflects the blue sky.

I feel at peace here, even with the aching in my muscles. The wind pushes back my hair in a caressing touch.

I take a reverent step, and my eyes spot a girl at the edge of the pond. She lies on her front in a bright yellow dress, resting there daintily, her hair in springy curls and her plump frame exuding a feminine grace. I think her rather pretty, and catch myself enraptured. Her eyes look on dreamily over a patch of assorted flowers, as if in a daze, swinging her legs out behind her in an absentminded, rocking motion.

I feel an immediate and unexplainable urge to talk to her, and I pause, that tug on my heart getting the better of me. I clear my throat, trying not to appear too awkward.

She starts, clumsily coming to her feet, clasping her hands against the folds of her dress, but her eyes meet mine with intensity, even as they waver in their gaze.

I smile at her politely, doing my best to reassure her. I hope I did not startle her. She still looks so lovely, especially with her curls, parting over her delicate ears and falling over her round cheeks.

She clasps her hands, before looking up, her light cornflower eyes, dappled in sunlight, flashing back at mine.

"My name is Liela," I offer steadily, a pleasant note to my voice.

Her face brightens and I think she looks rather nice like that. "My name is Myllia," she says a bit breathlessly, then looks down. That brief earnestness turns to modesty.

"I'm glad to meet you, Myllia."

She looks to her hands, pinching her fingers together. "I was wondering if I would meet someone else here, but I thought another person would be hard to find." Her eyes turn up to meet mine.

"I thought I could take some time for a walk. I don't think I have ever been to this courtyard, so meeting you is more by chance." I glance around. "This is a pretty place. What are you doing here?"

"Well, that is something I want you to find out." She flutters her eyelashes at me, but a moment later, her eyes wander elsewhere, unfocused.

What does she mean by that? I wonder. She's a bit of a strange girl, but her words are mesmerizing.

"Not to pry, but you don't look like someone who would stop to see me, not that I mind ... You can forget I said that. She grips her dress tightly, her lips pursed. "You look ... never mind." She shakes her head. "You are from the nobility too, aren't you? A Lady? That is what most of the people around here are. You dress a little differently than most do though."

I look more closely at her. Yes, she must be a Lady. I smile courteously. "I am." For a moment, I am at a loss, stumbling over my words in her presence. "I am ... a Lord, really."

She covers her mouth with her hand. "I can say that sounds better on you."

My cheeks feel hot.

"Are you tired, Liela?"

I chuckle, thinking of Father again. "A little."

Her breath grows unsteady for a moment, like she really wants to say something. "I want ..." She puts a hand to her chest, smiling apologetically.

"Myllia?" I reach out, taking a tentative step.

"Do not bother." She grows quiet, twisting at her dress, fingers white.

I begin to worry that I made her too nervous by approaching her, but I press her lightly. "Is there something you want?"

"Well ..." She meets my eyes with a growing certainty. "This may seem a bit forward of me, but I was wondering ... Could I be your friend?"

I blink, caught off guard at her directness, before forming a reassuring, kind smile. "Of course." I find that I do want that. Maybe because of Father's words or because there's something that makes me like her, drawing me to stay. My heartbeat quickens. It is the same impulse that drew me here in the first place. And I find that it's hard for my eyes to leave her. I can see the small exhale of relief from her lips, and I cannot help but let a short chuckle escape me. "You're peculiar, Myllia."

"I suppose I am." Myllia's cheeks flush as she turns her eyes away. "I just like you. Maybe we just met, but I wanted you to know that."

My heart pounds for a moment and my mouth feels dry. I don't understand why, it just does.

"So ... I thought I would ask to be your friend. Maybe it does not make sense, but it does to me. Sometimes, I think that is all that matters."

I give a weak smile. "Maybe it is, but I don't think I would know. You seem like a unique person."

"I would not say that." She looks back to me, dimples forming on her soft cheeks.

With clarity in her eyes, she reaches for my hand. Her grip is surprisingly firm, and I try to hide my surprise as I hold her hand delicately.

Her words and actions seem unexpectedly intense. I don't object, and she pulls me over to the pond, sitting gracefully in a patch of daisies, under the boughs of the tree in the courtyard, her daffodil-yellow dress spreading out beneath her.

I follow suit, with more practiced movements, elegant in their own right, but with a stiffer, more militant air.

Myllia stares out at the pond for a moment, and I wonder what is going on in her head.

I break the silence, trying to alleviate this feeling of awkwardness. "How old are you, Myllia?"

"I just turned nineteen a month ago," she says with reserved grace, plucking at a daisy, the arms of her dress trailing the grass enchantingly.

"That is my age as well!" My heart swells. I know I should not feel this way, but somehow, I like sharing that between us.

"You look older—I mean," she rushes to say, her eyes flickering over me, "in a mature way."

"What do you mean by that?" I ask with a laugh.

She giggles softly. "Nothing. You just look a little serious. You are a little too poised and stiff."

"Oh ..." I am suddenly very aware of myself. Goosebumps form on my skin as I make an effort to relax.

"What I mean is ... I like it. You look very ... dignified," she adds, touching her fingers gently to her cheek.

I try to relax my shoulders, and she laughs heartily. I feel hot all of a sudden, but I cannot help laughing at myself. A weight lifts off my chest.

"Liela, I was just teasing." Myllia's smile widens. I want to ask why you stopped to talk to me … but I think I will let that sit in my mind some. Likewise, I think the same of me asking to be your friend." There is a soft glow in her eyes.

"All right, Myllia." I give a short laugh.

"You are a soldier? Is that right? Not just nobility." Her fingers come up to her jawline in curiosity. "I know—it is probably obvious."

"Yes, I am. I always aspired to that …" My hands settle comfortably over my lap. "It is a dream, to protect my sister and everyone I love. I suppose it might seem a lot to aspire to, but that is what I have always reached for." I look up over the stonework of the rising towers with a smile playing over my lips. "That is the goal and the path I set for myself." I know it may sound ludicrous and certainly not something that should bring me peace, but it does.

She shakes her head, looking at me in awe and admiration. "No—that sounds weighty, Liela." She places an emphasis on my name and my back tingles. Her eyes turn elsewhere, distant for a moment. I dwell on that, but decide to keep my concerns to myself, for now.

"I suppose it is, but I will gladly do it, if it means I can protect my sister." I think of Dunet with an obvious affection coming over my features, and I turn my head to glance at our tower, looking up blissfully in the summer air, so far up above my head.

"I bet she is proud to have you as a sister. What is her name?" Myllia asks tenderly.

"Her name is Dunet. I think you would like her."

"Her name is really pretty. I would love to meet her sometime."

"Maybe I will bring her, at some point," I say with growing excitement.

"Please, do. You know, Liela ..." She hesitates for a moment, with a glance down, and then looks back at my eyes. "You have a pretty name too."

I feel a slight tingling in my cheeks and dismiss her compliment with a light laugh. "Anyway, Myllia, I think you should tell me about yourself."

She looks distant again, swishing her fingers over the grass. "I do not think there is much to tell, really."

"Do you want to try?" And I hold that curiosity in my voice, for I am genuinely interested. I do wonder whether I should be pushing her, but my curiosity gets the better of me.

She ponders this, looking dreamy, her hand paused over the grass. "I spend too much time thinking about nothing really. Outside my lessons, I enjoy going for walks and stopping to take everything in. I like the flowers here and the shade of the leaves. They are really quite beautiful ..." Her eyes play familiarly over the scenery, her tone a misty contemplation. "I have tried my hand at a few pastimes"—her eyes fall—"but I never really saw the point. I come here quite often. I find it quaint."

"That does not sound like nothing. If anything, you sound rather thoughtful. And I can see why you like it here," I say as I turn my eyes over the peaceful courtyard.

"Thank you, and maybe it is not." Her eyes turn to me with a flicker, even though their shine seems to melt away with her coming words. "But I really don't think I am all that interesting."

I shake my head. "From what I can see, you're a sweet person, Myllia."

"I appreciate it, Liela." It is like a small flush comes over her face. The wind dances lightly in the soft tendrils of her hair.

"Do you want to tell me about your family, Myllia?" I ask, since I had already talked about my sister.

"I suppose." She looks up at the flowers distractedly. "My parents are … well." She shrugs. "They are largely absent from my life. I have studied and practiced being a lady … but other than that, they don't care what I do. For now, at least. I suppose that is why I spend so much time alone, daydreaming. There is not much else I feel I can do."

I feel a gap in my chest, my fingers clenching in the grass as they sprawl out behind me, but my face remains controlled, showing my compassion for her. "I think you deserve more, Myllia. They're lucky to have a daughter like you."

"Maybe, but there is nothing I can do about it." Her voice is resigned, her face passive. "Anyway, I would rather talk about you. Can we?"

"Are you sure?" I ask, an ache in my words that reaches out to her. I hope she will accept my offer to listen.

"I am fine with it. I really am. But ... maybe another time ..." Her voice trails off with a soft clasp at my heart, and her eyes lighten up as she smiles at me with that same pretty smile.

I do what she asks, as I want what she feels she needs. "Well, I suppose you likely know my family name, Cordre. Liela Fiera Cordre—older daughter and future Lord of Claralis, if my sister does not take that title. Hopefully, Commander regardless," I say with a small bit of dramatic emphasis—unusual for me, but a small part of myself feels like showing my pride.

Myllia puts her hand to her mouth. "Wow, Liela!"

Grinning, I lower my head. "I apologize, if that is a lot to handle." I turn modest again, feeling a bit too showy for my own comfort.

"I think you live up to your title. Your name did sound familiar."

"I suppose now you know why."

"Yes, but I am glad I met you, regardless. Your title does not matter to me, but your citizens are lucky to have someone with such a beautiful heart."

I feel an incredible heat come into my cheeks, and I have trouble collecting myself for once. "I am glad you think so." I try to clear my head at my momentary lightheadedness. My eyes drift to her curls, falling over her soft, rounded cheeks and the fair whites of her ears. A moment later, it occurs to me to wonder what time it is, and I look up at where the sun sits in the sky. I try to act casual again. "Anyway, Myllia, I think it's time that I leave. I want to see you again, though," I say, a sureness rippling through my mind: what I said is true, even if I seem to be in an unnecessary hurry.

I find a brilliant smile on her lips; she is seemingly unfazed at my abruptness. "I will be waiting here again for you, Liela." She looks pleased and happy, and I cannot help but feel that same blossoming feeling.

A Friend and Nothing More

Liela

I tuck Dunet in as I finish combing the gentle waves of her buttery hair. She wrinkles her eyebrows at me. "Where are you going?"

I smile at her, my hand resting on my knee as I sit on the edge of the bed. "To go see a puppy." I try making light of it—or Darnor, though I am sure he would not mind. But it's fun, and unfortunately true, to draw that parallel of him recently.

Dunet springs forward. "I want to go!"

I push her back gently into the fluffiness of her pillows. She sinks into the bedsheets. "Not that kind of puppy," I chide.

"Then ... what kind?" She scrunches her nose, her hands kneading at the blankets in curiosity.

"One that chased a girl everywhere," I reply smoothly, glossing over the truth. I try not to discuss any of my engagement letters from various lords with Dunet; I don't know how to approach it with her, especially with how young she is. I suppose there is a lot that I don't want to talk about with her. I like keeping everything light and fun. To her, my duty may not even be that serious, but she does know that it matters to me a great deal.

"I would love that!" Dunet's eyes brighten. "Did the girl not love the puppy?"

I take a deep breath, looking intently at the ceiling. "She did love him, but not enough to let him drool all over her all the time." I draw out my words with an exasperated half-smile.

"I think he is cute! I would keep him all to myself!" Dunet chortles with an uptilt of her head.

"I'm sure you would, because you're kind." I know I probably would too, if I were younger, though in Dunet's line of thought, of course. I wish I could see it that rosily. "He would make a good puppy," I mutter with an eye roll and then break out laughing.

Dunet cocks her head. "What is it?"

"Nothing, Dunet. Now get to bed." I glance out the window at the darkening sky, pulling the sheets back up over her shoulders. I kiss her forehead, then I step over to draw the white-and-pearl embroidered curtains closed. Turning to leave the room with a hesitant step, I notice that her eyes are still following me innocently. Then they disappear from my vision as I leave the room.

I take a walk over the walls of the castle, the stars of dusk bristling through the chilly air. The lights of our tower shine nearby; flecks of hearth fire into the night. The central gardens lie to either side of the narrow wall, sprawling out from the castle's center.

And standing there, on the wall above the gardens, is Darnor.

With a decisive purpose in my stride, I finally decide to stop avoiding him. Up until this point, I had used my schedule as a pretext, but it is hard to use forever. Darnor is a friend, but at times he can get a little clingy for my liking. We have always been the best of friends, but this feels like a distance I would rather avoid. I had hoped that stepping away would solve our friendship, because of my aversion to confrontation. It never poses a problem during my duties, because I understand that confrontation is simply something I must do, but this is different. I find it hard to bring myself into these personal conversations. I usually end up brushing them off.

I make sure to relax my shoulders, putting on a cheerful smile and clearing up my eyes. My fingers trace the gaps and rises in the stonework, for a solid grounding. "Lord Darnor Veln!" I lay out in a bright enough greeting, trying to play the slight edge out of my voice.

Darnor leans against the wall. He has elegant brown hair, deep blue eyes, a slightly pointed nose, a pleasant face, and a frame that is relatively thin, but still well-muscled. While his voice is mild, I sense an underlying taughtness, his arms tense near his sides. "You don't have to be quite so formal," he jokes.

I give a small laugh, a bit more conscious of his curious gaze than usual. "I am glad, Darnor. It's good to see you." And that does bring a genuine warmth, despite the steady prickling at my mind.

"You have been busy." With a light, steady look, he relaxes his posture and leans away from the balcony. "Or, at least, that is what your father keeps saying." He flashes a grin.

"Yes, you know how it is." Though, I could have spared some time. I am grateful for my father's cover up. For the most part, it's true that I have been busy, and I wish Darnor would waste his efforts on someone else. I honestly don't think he can tell how exhausting this is. He has seemed tense lately and I think I know why. I never wanted anything different with him, just the friendship we have. But, of course, I am afraid of laying that out. Sooner or later, I will have to find someone, assuming I lead the city and not Dunet. It is expected of me, of course, but not yet, if I can help it. I finally lose a bit of my patience. This was going to happen eventually, and it might as well be now. "There's something on your mind, is there not, Darnor?"

He shifts slightly, his eyes straying from mine and his lips pursing. Whether this is in thought or distaste, I don't know.

But I find that even now, I want to be patient with him. He is one of my best friends after all, alongside Dunet, Driena, and Myllia.

"Liela." He pauses, glancing at me meaningfully. "I am a lord, in title, if not in age and mind. My parents expect things of me and ... we are close." He places extra emphasis on the word close. It comes off rather roundabout. "Liela, I want your hand in marriage."

I force myself to consider it for just a moment, even though I already know my answer. He is just a friend and I want it to stay that way. I feel no attraction to him; love, yes— a deep warmth of affection, but only as friends. And because he is my friend, I want him to know that. I sigh and give him a small smile. "I am sorry, Darnor, but I don't want what you want. You're my friend and always will be, but nothing more." A small, icy thread runs itself through my mind at the thought of losing him, but I trust him more than that.

A look of disappointment crosses over his face for just a moment, before it is gone, and he returns the smile, even with a hint of relief, his shoulders sinking with a pent-up exhale. "Then it will stay that way. Liela"—he meets my eyes truthfully— "I am sorry for asking it of you."

A gentle breeze dissipates from my mind as well. I close my eyes, knowing that, despite Darnor's faults, I picked a good friend. "It's all right, Darnor. You know, you worried me, but I am glad you told me. Thank you." I flash him a mischievous grin. "And ... I suppose I should apologize for avoiding you." Maybe it is somewhat to get away from my awkwardness, but I just want to joke with him too.

He feigns astoundment, his eyes wide. "So, you really were avoiding me? I should have known!"

"Thanks to Father, I could."

He laughs merrily at that. "You two are too similar!"

"I know we are. Like me, he allows himself to tolerate you."

"And I hope you will continue to. But, Liela" —he turns serious again— "there's no reason you should apologize for avoiding me. I was ..." His fist clenches, as he looks at the ground. "Out of my bounds. You clearly did not want it." He looks up, shaking his head. "And, regardless, you have a lot going on. It was ... uncalled for ..."

"Maybe it was, but ... Darnor, you're my best friend after Dunet and Driena, of course. You know that?" I try to act light about it, but this does mean a lot to me.

He nods solemnly. "I do. I really do. And it does mean a lot to me. It means more to me than what I asked for. I don't want you to think otherwise."

"Then promise me not to act all weird around me again." I try acting casual, but a strained edge still lingers in my voice. "But by all means, do it as much as you would like around Father."

"Of course, and I promise to provide your father some company."

"He would appreciate it." I breathe in again and then force out a prying breath. "So, how have you been?"

"Excellent!" he says with rising spirits. "Or as excellent as I could find myself, in my position, though it may not be too different from yours, except I think you're more committed."

"Fortunately, I am. And fortunately, I believe in you too."

"I would not be so sure of that, but I will take the compliment. How about your sister? Is she ... dealing with everything all right? I know that was worrying you."

It is, and I want to believe that she is coping. Sometimes I feel like I am forcing myself to, the walls I built blocking everything else out. I hesitate. "Better than I thought she would, not that I expected less. It's just ... a lot of pressure. I don't think I can ever not be worried. I always make time for her." My smile turns wistful. "She is a ray of sunshine, as she always is, though she lets me know how bored she is without me." I laugh at the memory. It warms my heart, even as I feel a souring twinge.

Darnor's face turns pensive as he poses his hand under his chin. I know he cares deeply, and wants the best for my relationship with my sister. "I really hope she is, but she sounds like she is lonely without you."

My heart sinks. "That is what I am afraid of. The castle staff all love her, of course, but they're busy. She tells me she has friends, but she never brings them over. I worry that her position is too much of a barrier. She is animated all the time when I am around her, so I know she is happy."

Darnor looks at me with a spark and a slight snap of his fingers. "Maybe you could ask Myllia to take care of her?" I had told Darnor about her several months ago. "She isn't her age, but I know you two are close. She could look after her some, since she has a lot of time, as I understand it. From what you told me about her, she would not mind."

"Yes, she could," I reply, a flutter in my voice. I had not thought of that. They really are similar, in at least a few ways. Maybe Myllia could provide her more company? Something about imagining the two of them together just feels right, and thinking about her, I realize that Dunet has never met Myllia. Why had I not introduced them? "Thank you, Darnor. I think I will introduce them sometime." I trail off in a daze, my heart in a distant-seeming courtyard.

"I know she will love her."

"She will," I say surely. Then, I pause, thinking I should ask him a bit more, as I try keeping my thoughts in the present, rather than with Myllia. "Anyway, do you have a lot of work?"

"Yes, a great deal of lecturing, courtesy of my dear tutor!"

"Nothing new, then?" I reply slyly.

"Not particularly. I confess that it is getting on my nerves somewhat." He sighs.

"Well, I suppose I may just feel sorry for you," I send a teasing look at him.

"Not likely," comes a disbelieving laugh. "It could be worse."

"Then there's nothing new with you."

"Not really." Darnor shrugs.

"Any love rivals you have to worry about?" I prod with a lofty air, feeling a pleasantness again around Darnor again, for the most part. "Now that I am gone, they should be all over you."

He gives a charming laugh at that, rocking nonchalantly on his heel. "Unfortunately, yes, though I am not sure that it's me, so much as my station."

"A pity. You actually are not half bad." I raise my eyebrows.

"Is that a compliment?" he asks crisply.

"Do you think I would be friends with you otherwise?"

He shakes his head in deflation. "I suppose not."

I give a crooked grin, resting my elbows over the wall, fists on my chin. "Driena?"

He takes a short step back. "Of course not."

"I thought so ..." I imply with raised eyebrows.

"You know how much she annoys me."

"I very much do," I quip.

"Not funny, Liela." He stares at me darkly.

"All right." I deflate a bit. "I suppose that wasn't fair." Honestly, though, it would make my chest burst to have my two best friends as partners. Sometimes, I get a little ahead of myself with them. It isn't like me. I want to respect him, too. I shift my weight back. "Well, my lord, I think I had best get on to bed."

He opens his eyes wide, in mock shock. "Well, then." His voice softens. "Sorry for keeping you up. And, Liela," he says, clearing his throat, "remember: there's no need for the lord."

I roll my eyes. "That may be so. Anyway, I may just see you tomorrow." I start walking away. He turns, giving me a wave goodnight. And I wave back, releasing all my remaining tension in a breath and then grinning warmly. I do very much still hope to see him.

A Circle to Ground You

Liela

I walk next to Driena on my lunch break, hearing the sounds of training from the fences to the right, beside the two-tiered facility of the barracks on the back side of the castle. This facility faces the direction of the Kalltarris Mountains, over the plains in the distance. The barracks stand imposing and glorious in the mountains' shadow, but simple: a small fortress near the outer wall, guards over the first tier, going in and out onto the main castle walls. Swords crash and stutter in a droning din from the grounds. Farther in, many of the knights study their academics between their training, propped against trees, sprawled on the lawn, or under bushes in the small park on the back side of the castle. That park presents itself almost like a mini forest, opening to a lawn and then the dirt of the practice area.

"You were brilliant as always, Liela," comes Driena's pretty bell voice, but with an air of command always under its surface. She is respectable, if a little more open with me and Darnor.

"Driena, really, I could use a little less praise." I often feel this way. "From you, least of all. You know I want you at my side, not behind me."

"Of course, Liela, but that does not eliminate the fact that you were." Her eyes flash in an exalting brightness, before scanning over the tree line. "Oh, look who it is," she scoffs lightly.

"Lord Darnor Veln," I say in a lilting whisper.

"When will this lord catch us a break?"

"When we stop gracing him with our presence. I think it is because he likes you too."

"I thought he proposed to you."

"Irrelevant." I brush it off. "And no ... I think you misunderstand that I do not like him."

"And probably no man."

I wonder if that is true, finding nothing pushing back at the notion. I have never felt anything that people would call attraction, when the other girls talk about boys. I view this as a strength. My mind flits through to another image, of a copper leaf in a courtyard, and I scrunch up my face, confused at my own drifting thoughts.

"What is it, Liela?"

I sigh. "Just tired, I think." I give her a playful look, then I push at her back.

She gives me an intense look, then turns to Darnor. "A pleasure to see you today, Darnor." She crosses her arms over her chest.

He looks unfazed. "Could I join you for lunch?"

"Why certainly, it's not like we asked," she says, an aloof smirk on her face. It is fake, of course, because Darnor is a most sincere friend. I mean, he really is, but I catch myself giving an eye roll.

"But we were waiting for him anyway," I insert.

"Shut up, Liela," she snaps lightly, shielding her face from a laugh.

Darnor is, of course, the third in my main friend group—Driena, Darnor, and myself. It's laid-back, joking, and pleasant. I love them both. If I did not have Dunet, we could be close enough to be siblings. We jab at each other, frequently, but it's all in good fun. "Did you get out of your studies all right, Darnor?"

He sags his shoulders. "I hardly did."

"I wish you would study harder, Darnor." Driena eyes him. "But ... I may be glad you got out."

"It's never as boring as I make it out to be. I actually do like it half the time."

"Pity," she drawls.

"Say, Darnor, Driena, how about we find our usual spot?" I suggest.

"Yes, why of course, Liela." Driena falls into step beside me. "It's quite a nice day for sitting outside." She tilts her head back. "Almost like a late-summer picnic."

I agree with her. I can hear the incessant drone of the insects and the occasional muted chirpings of the birds that sets my own heart in a gentle song. The light pink rose bushes and honeysuckles sit up against the wall and around the trees, the bees buzzing around them lazily. I feel a pleasant sinking of my eyelids, before snapping myself back out of my daze. "Are we studying today too, Darnor?"

"I brought my book. I figured we could catch up together."

"Or we could just keep up in the first place," Driena adds, without looking at him.

He gives a flustered smile. "Maybe you're right?"

"I thought so, but I know I would hate to see you fall behind either way, Darnor. You're much too bright for that, trust me."

We stop by several rose bushes under a sprawling tree, the castle walls rising at our backs. Here, we have a wide view of the grounds.

I move to sit back, knees pulled close to my chest, propped up with my arms. Darnor lazes back across from me, and Driena lowers herself tenderly down next to me.

Darnor flips open his book. "Not right away!" Driena hisses, reaching over to close the book.

Darnor shuts it with a muffled snap. "I apologize. That wasn't very courteous of me."

I reach into my pack, pulling out a sandwich— tomatoes, spinach, and a hummus spread.

Darnor snaps his eyes to it momentarily, as he opens his own pack.

I cut off a third, handing it to Driena, who grins at Darnor. "He gets one too," I announce to her with a prodding look.

"Of course, he does," Driena mutters.

"Well, the two of you are tied for best friend after Dunet."

Driena sinks back, turning her head. "I suppose. Darnor, you could become a knight if you wanted, you know."

He pauses, looking at her with a hand in his bag. "True, but that isn't really like me. I trust it all to Liela."

"I mean, yes, I would too." She pauses intently. "No, you don't strike me that way." She sighs. "Though, I thought I might ask."

He picks up his own sandwich, passing me a piece and Driena one.

"Is your sister getting enough attention?" Driena draws herself up.

I stare at the sandwich, my stomach twisting. "I really hope so." I really hope I can avoid this lecture, even if well-intentioned. It does drag at my heart. But Driena's concern still lifts me up in comfort, somewhat.

Her face softens. "I think she understands everything. I just wanted to make sure everything was okay with the two of you. She is getting older, so tell us if you need help." She turns her gentle eyes on me. "If you think about it, she isn't really that much different than any other girl."

I nod solemnly, as if tracing the motion. "You have a sister too. Right, Driena?" I already know the answer, so of course, there's no reason to ask, but I feel a prickle in my voice.

"Ella, she is a little older than yours. She is maturing well, and she has taken up a preoccupation in tailoring." She shakes her head. "I just am glad we can still get along, much better than we used to. If anything, I think that will be the case with both of you."

Maybe I do feel a tension at that? How could things be better than how they are? Dunet is perfect. I smile. She is more wondrous and carefree than any flower.

"Be glad you're the oldest." Darnor clears his throat.

"Oh, sorry, Darnor," Driena says with a bite of her lip, eyes flashing dangerously. "I forgot how hard that was for you." Driena goes silent, turning back to me. Darnor does his best to hide the falling of his eyes, though I would not blame him.

"But I keep thinking, what will I do with my mother?" I shift the sandwich in my fingers, pursing my lips. "I just wonder how that will affect Dunet." My skin crawls. I wonder how it will land when she notices our tension.

"Liela," Driena chides. "You're thinking too far into it, and all for the wrong reasons. Think about what you want, for once. That might help," she settles her voice soothingly.

My chest deflates in a deep sigh, mind wandering aimlessly. That is the problem: that I don't know what to do with my relationship with my mother. But with Dunet, for Dunet, I do. I know I do. "I know what I want, Driena," I say with a touching look.

"Do you?" I can see her eyebrows furrow. "Because I wonder if you push things too far sometimes."

I shake my head, feeling the risings of bile at this maze in my heart that I refuse to enter. "I don't quite understand."

"I mean, and while I cannot read your mind ..." She slows down. "Can you be certain you are being honest with your feelings towards Dunet?"

I freeze for a moment, and look away furtively.

"Driena," Darnor retorts, a small, searing shard to his words. "you know she is. Liela is the most honest, dedicated sister I know. Yes, you had fights with your sister and your family, but that does not mean Liela will go through that." He raises his hands, his eyes softening as his voice settles. "And I am not saying that your family is any worse."

"I know, Darnor. I appreciate it. I just wanted to make her think about it, for her sister's good ... and her own." Her voice lowers, but is still gentle and kind. She looks directly at me. "I thought I was a good sister. I thought I was a good daughter. I was ..." She swallows with a tremble. "I was neither, and I needed to be. I wanted to be." Her hands start shaking as she tries grounding them in the grass.

Darnor's face turns ashen. He takes her hand in a comforting motion. "Driena, you don't need to be that hard on yourself. You were always much better than that. But ... that was a little harsh."

"I see where you're coming from, Driena. Dunet always seems so happy, though ... I am afraid that if I reach further ... I break that." I feel at a loss. Not broken, because I push away Driena's words with utter conviction, but a sliver of her words rests heavy in my mind.

Driena sighs. "Of all the girls in the world, Liela ..." Her smile lightens. "You're too soft. And Darnor, thank you. Yes, I have come to the point in realizing that I am too hard on myself, but the point is that it happened, and I changed." She draws her hand back. "And I suppose I have to thank you too, Darnor. You get the same praise of being a softy." Her eyes dance as they look at him.

"It's the least I can do." He grins.

"Now, Darnor, I suppose I will have to take you up on your offer of studying together." She shifts closer to him, pulling us into a more even circle. I wonder if there is another reason for her to draw closer to him. I can see the way they look at each other. If there is, I like it for her. She deserves it.

Both of them really are kind. That is why I appreciate them so much. If I ever need help and I have the courage to reach out, I know they will be there.

Driena and I walk down the fence line and into the musky shed-like room at the tail-end of the barracks.

She gets there first, grabbing a practice sword and balancing it experimentally. She hands it to me with a smile of comradery. "For you, Liela," she says, her voice chivalrous.

"Thank you, Driena." I grip it, perfectly balanced. She knows me too well and I feel a tingle in my eyes.

She grabs one of her own and we move back into the sunlight, facing each other in the square fencing.

Driena stands there, as if painted against the Kalltarris Mountains. I note how pretty she looks, facing me in her slender silver-plated armor strapped over her violet tunic and black tights. Her silver-flecked, river-blue eyes meet mine in challenge, with the uptilt of her head, dark hair tied in a ponytail and fluttering in the breeze.

I take a moment to glance at Darnor, who is leaning against the fence, next to all the knights. A lord indeed—I roll my eyes—here to see his two best friends fight.

I shift my eyes back to Driena, breathing in steadily.

She lowers her sword, stepping over gracefully to meet me, hair still billowing like a dark angel. She is a brilliant force on the battlefield, made all the more potent with her intelligence and her speed. She is nearly my equal.

Nearly.

There is a reason Commander Wheln favors me, but I always will want Driena by my side, regardless.

She strikes, whirling her sword through the air, and I can see her eyes calculating her next move.

I block at her next flurry, bracing my sword and maneuvering in a jab.

She swipes at it meticulously, and I redirect it into a cut. Though she has smoothly turned out of my reach, I still manage to pull in closer and cut inwards.

I duck, pulling back and breathing heavily, looking for an opening. Then I press forward, with an uppercut, striking against her sword. As she pulls back, she takes a quick sweep at my legs.

I avoid this by stepping back. Then, going in again, I concentrate on her left side and she deflects my blow, as if on instinct, and jabs at my shoulder. However, my sword up in a blink, and pushes back at her.

I press a few strokes, trying to overwhelm her, before moving back to the defensive.

She tries a move I recognize, a jab and then feigning a redirection, only to continue.

I grasp that moment, twisting at her wrist, and drive my sword just short of her armor, pausing it there.

She looks up with a tight, but good-natured smile, just as remarkable as her performance. "Nice job, Liela."

"You deserve it too." I grin, lowering my sword.

We walk back to the barracks storeroom and then make our way over to Darnor.

"Does the lord have to watch?" I laugh.

"I felt like sticking around," he says lazily.

"You always do." Driena puts her hand to her hip. "So, what did you think?"

"Nothing short of magnificent, though you let me down, Driena." He frowns at her.

"If I was fighting for you. I fight with Liela, for Liela." She looks at me with a gleaming appraisal.

"If I make it to commander, she will be my second."

"And, for avoiding praise, you seem to like putting it on me." She turns merrily.

"I do a little bit, which is only fair." I chuckle. "See, Darnor? You're missing out."

"To think I did not know!" He brushes out a laugh. "But I had better get back to my tutor. Back to your sister, Liela?"

"Yes, I think I will be heading there." I glance up, seeing that it is late afternoon leading into evening, the shadows starting to stretch. It pains me how much of my day I end up away from her.

"Tell her hello for me." He waves over his shoulder.

"Oh, she will be thrilled—and in laughter." I pick my voice up in a gentle pricking.

I can hear him sigh. "It does not sound like a story I want her to hear, but I suppose you will just have to embarrass me. Well then," he stutters just slightly, "goodbye, Driena."

"And I will see you tomorrow." She looks back at me with a glance. "Do you mind?"

"Not at all," I say casually.

She meets my eyes. "See you tomorrow, Liela." She then catches up with Darnor.

I roll my eyes and laugh. Today was a good day, but it isn't over just yet. I turn towards the castle, making my way back home and to Dunet waiting for me.

A Day to Pass the Time

Dunet

Without Liela, I feel like I am stuck in an empty pit; I want to feel her presence again, but find myself alone, having to work harder to keep my mind occupied. It feels a bit numbing, but I nevertheless twist myself into action.

I never let Liela know these feelings, because the fact that she will be back always brings sunbeams of happiness to my mind.

But there are morbid pieces of me I never share. I can manage them with Liela, though—enough that they never truly stick in my consciousness.

With her ... I have someone who clutches at me and pulls me close, no matter what.

No—I shake my head—I have the world when I am with her. I have myself when I am with her.

I rock back-and-forth on my bed, my smile cracking upright again.

Maybe I should go to the kitchens? My cheeks warm up. I love the kitchens! Chef Feln, Madam Pennella, Torie, Joanne, Marta, Ila, Geon, Kreenie, Lunan, Alnor—they make me feel so welcome, like a second family. The thought of them quells the internal, silent roaring through my otherwise jarring silence.

That decides it for me—that it's better than being in my room, waiting for Liela. I never know how long she will be gone. Halfern tutors me on most days, and my group lessons take place before that, but nothing today.

I roll over a few times, before landing with a thump on the fuzzy, white rug. I clutch my head, giggling a little.

I wish Liela would dote on me for that. She would have been worried.

But ... I also feel a slackening of my cheeks, knowing I don't have to deal with her sometimes intense attention.

And neither of these sit well, like a chilly touch. I wonder which is better ... or worse. I give my head a vigorous shake, bound to my feet, and run out into the hall. My bare feet skim over the cool carpet of morning. The cold makes me feel wide awake. I quickly peek into the dining room and find a note from Liela:

Dunet,

I had to leave early today. Father is busy, and Mother had to leave, too. I hope you like this. Have an adventure while I am gone! Take care, and I love you always.

- Liela

I put it down, a small rising of bile in my mouth and a deflation in my chest. Alone. But, I feel a bittersweet warmth at her note. I quickly shove down the steamed carrots and blackberries, then scoop from the bowl of lentil-spinach soup. Sister always makes sure to give me a little treat. She knows that I love carrots and blackberries more than anything else she can feed me.

The spoon clatters into the bowl as I finish, turning to go, but I halt halfway across the room, and I rush back. I want to at least be helpful and make things nice. I scurry to the sink, scrubbing at the bowl furiously, then I skid down the hall, my face brightening at the prospect of the kitchens.

The stairs swirl by in a blur, joined by the twinkling of the sun through the glass dome of the central room. I skip the remaining distance, still in my pale-blue nightgown, tinged in a soft-white hue.

At the edge of the spread kitchens, I stop to gaze around at the steam they produce, billowing and swirling around the glass ceiling. The bustle of everyone looks inviting and occupying.

Prancing over, I spot Chef Feln. I tug at the back of his white apron.

"Lady Dunet!" he exclaims merrily, a soft rumble in his voice. He kneels, the short curls of his red hair sparking a familiar image from under his chef's hat, deep dimples and dark freckles in his dough-white skin.

"Good morning, Thomas!" It is the name everyone uses for him in the kitchens. It makes my head swirl that I can use it too. I break out in a grin, tapping my pointer fingers together and looking at him with my eyes peeled back. "Umm ... I would like to help!"

"Of course!" he says, then points to the sink. "Go wash up over there, if you would not mind."

I nod vigorously, making sure to please him. A moment later, he moves over purposely to Torie, Kreenie, and Lunan, and my heart leaps excitedly. I love them! I love all of them really, but … Torie is my favorite. They're all so fun! They're the youngest in the kitchens, all in their teens and a few years younger than Liela—15 for Kreenie, Lunan is 16, and Torie is 17. All of them are still learning, not yet professional cooks, but I know that they're basically skilled enough to be. Thomas lets them train here and it does sound so fun!

Kreenie skips over to get me as I wash my hands, hers laced behind her back, brown pigtails bouncing in the heat, tied with bright pink and red ribbons. Beneath her work apron, she wears a pink and gray plaid suit-styled top above a bright yellow skirt, which stops just above her knees. I can make out her knee-high white and purple socks under that, but my eyes are drawn to her face as a smile swells on her lips and her fun, hazel eyes light on me.

"Dunet!" she offers her hand to me and spins me around in greeting. I giggle uncontrollably at the sudden movement, my breath leaving me in dizziness. She takes both my hands and says, "Come with me!" Her voice bounces up an octave. I like her second, after Torie. She is the most erratically fun of them all, her bouncing energy and loose, playful smile so inviting. She stares at my feet as we prance. "Can you follow?" she asks, working herself up into a scattered rhythm.

I try to, giggling again, and almost fall.

She puts a steady hand on my back, looking around furtively. "Careful."

Torie preens at me kindly as I get closer. "Dunet, you look lovely today!" She walks over, her voice softening in familiarity. "I missed you." Her auburn hair is pulled straight back from her forehead, held by a black headband. Her flower earrings compliment the kind smile she adorns, as do her dark-blue eyes and the rest of her soft features. Her thin frame is covered in a simple, black long-sleeved shirt and pants, with a trim of violet along the arms.

"I missed you too!" I jump, feeling as though I could soar.

She reaches forward, parting my hair back and placing a sky-blue hair clip to the left side of my forehead. "There, now you look even lovelier!"

"She looked better as a bedhead," Kreenie bemoans. "It lets all the fun out!"

Torie contemplates this, looking at me with a serene gaze. "True, but I think she looks cute. Do you feel like that, Dunet?"

"I do!" My voice lifts in awe. I feel a fluffiness around her. Nothing like I do with Liela, but ... light, in a different way. Though I feel a little guilty, knowing that she reminds me of Liela. I glance at Kreenie, hoping she doesn't take it too hard.

"Are you ready to help today?" Torie's hands fold behind her back.

"I really want to!"

Lunan comes up next to me, having a short staring contest with Kreenie before he passes me some dough from behind his back, and gives me a sidelong glance with his bright blue eyes. "For you, miss." His ashen hair looks neat over his sparse eyebrows, framing his delicate, white skin.

I stifle a giggle. It comes out as a snort, as I meet his eyes. I want to say thank you, but I fear taking sides. I feel myself pull a bit closer to him—he always treats me so nicely. Kreenie said once that he treated me "Like a Lady, except with ulterior motives!" Everyone else at the table had laughed at that. I had laughed too, because I thought I should. Sometimes when I don't know what to do, I follow other people.

Torie usually gets me out of confusing situations. As much as I like Kreenie, half the time I stumble when responding to her, and sometimes I have trouble responding to Lunan too, even though he tries to help me. Their words don't always make sense. A lot of peoples' words don't make sense to me, and I often want to shrink back when asked questions.

"No fair!" Kreenie stammers. "You spoil her, Lunan." Her arms cross under her brimming chest as she looks down at him with a face that could only look comical on her.

"You spoil her more. I think we can all give her some later." He holds his palms placatively upright. "How does that sound, Dunet?" He turns a calm, welcoming look back at me.

I look down, wanting to be polite. "You don't have to do anything for me." Sometimes it is overwhelming to be doted on, but I do long for the attention. It makes me feel included and loved.

"Both of you—you're making her nervous." Torie comes forward, taking my hand. "I think we should settle down and start cooking."

Kreenie bounces after us, unfazed. "Okay!"

Lunan trots beside us too, a pleasant smile on his lips.

Torie stops at one of the tables along the wall. "Dunet, can you get me a few things from the pantry?"

"Of course!"

"I expected nothing less." She hands me a list and I take it in both hands, scrunching my forehead.

"Do you think you can find these?"

I look back up at her, eyes wavering just past hers. "Yes." It comes out weakly. It would tear at me to disappoint her.

She looks me up and down, smiling with calm, unfaltering eyes that lift me up. "Would you like me to come with you?"

I hesitate for a moment, looking over my shoulder at the pantry across the room. I don't want to ask her.

"Here." She takes my hand and I clutch at it tightly, but enough not to hurt her. "I will come with you."

I feel cradled, clinging to her side as we cross the room. But I still feel small as I look around, despite my familiarity with the kitchens.

Torie opens the door. "Now, time for hide-and-seek!" She kneels, whispering in my ear. "Ready?" Her voice prods me forward.

I scurry around, grabbing the items that I am familiar with and relying on Torie for the others. She lifts me to a few shelves, and I love floating there.

I look back as she reaches up to a shelf that towers above me, even while on my tiptoes. She casts a fond smile back at me and says, "Now, time to go. Thank you for your help, Dunet."

She hands me a basket and I stuff the ingredients inside, heading across the floor with her.

I set my basket next to Torie's on the counter.

Kreenie taps my shoulder. "Would you like to help me?"

"What would you like me to help you with?" My hands clench in front of me, begging to help with anything.

"The most fun job of all!" She looks to Torie, who sighs, but nevertheless smiles. "Kreenie, there is nothing that says I am in charge."

Kreenie grabs my wrist, tugging me into a whiz across the room. "And off we go!"

My eyelids droop a little, and I feel the insistence of a tiny yawn, but these sensations are overshadowed by my sense of ease and energy that I could help. My mind settles down as we all come back together for lunch.

Kreenie nods along next to me. "Pass me the cheese!" She reaches for a plate of cheeses in the corner.

I know she is being rude. Liela would tell me to say please, and I would do it. I like pleasing people, so I don't quite understand her.

Alnor passes her some—he is an older man with a shaggy beard and eyes starting to sag, but a kindly expression on his face. I try to meet his eyes and smile, thankful that he met Kreenie's demand.

Kreenie takes the cheese in a frenzy, before giving a dip of her head, albeit fashionably. She looks down at it with a famished look, but she turns to me, asking "Want some?"

I pluck at a bit of the cheese, biting down. "It tastes delicious! Thank you, Kreenie!"

"No problem!" She shrugs it off with exuberance. "Joanne, Torie, Lunan, want some?" she insists, sliding the plate forward.

I find myself confused at Kreenie's opposing behaviors. My eyes dart quickly between the four of them, then I smile uncertainly at Kreenie.

Lunan takes a piece, studying it between his fingers. "I applaud your half-decent manners, but thank you, Kreenie." He pops it into his mouth. "Spicy."

Torie motions to Joanne, who takes a piece. Joanne is a woman in her thirties—silvery-blond hair on a pointed, crisp face. "Why, thank you." She says, clearly talking to a younger member of the kitchen, but with patience. She shifts back, taking another for Alnor, by her side—a tall, lanky man, with sandy brown hair swept to both sides of his head. They sit a bit apart from us. Torie, Kreenie, and Lunan sit together—a noticeable separation, but they're still very much an accepted part of the group.

My eyes follow them, as I finally process it all. I feel reassured as Torie motions to Kreenie.

"You first, Torie." Kreenie waves her hand.

Torie takes her cheese on her fork. "I think you waited long enough, Kreenie."

Kreenie reaches forward, plopping a piece in her mouth. Then, elbow on the table and knuckles on her chin, she makes a plucking noise and says, "Not bad! Salty."

I giggle at her reaction.

The whole time, my gaze had struggled to keep up with it all. I feel just on the verge of being a part of it.

"Say, Dunet, do you want anything else?" Kreenie asks.

"The artichokes, maybe," I say quickly, glancing at them.

Kreenie motions again, and this time Lunan reaches over. I squirm. A part of me feels wrong for having them do something for me, but I like that they are doing those things.

"Now, hold out your hands." Kreenie turns to me. "Plop!" she mouths as she drops it into my hands.

I stare at her and giggle, then I look around for approval.

"Kreenie, I think you will confuse her with your odd manners," Torie says.

Kreenie snags at her left pigtail, twirling it. "Oh, I think she gets it."

"I do!" I speak up, turning to her. "I think Kreenie is amazing," I splutter. While I don't understand everything, I do think that she is amazing.

"Well, I suppose I think so too." Lunan sinks back.

"Lunan." I twist at my fingers under the table. "I never thanked you for the dough."

He looks away. "Ah, that was nothing. But really, to work here, I think it's only fair to get a snack now and again."

Kreenie squeezes her arms around my waist as I sit on her lap. "We are here to take care of you." She looks down with a sparkle in her eyes.

Is that why? But … I always wonder if maybe I *am* causing trouble being here.

She boops me on the cheek with her finger. "No pouting, Dunet! We *are* your friends."

I giggle, pushing into her touch. "I know." I let those feelings wash away. "Kreenie, you remind me of something …" I trail off.

"A cat!" Lunan pulls forward.

Torie gives him a sidelong look. "You're right, Lunan, but you were far too quick at that."

"Well," he says, looking intently at his food, "it is a thought I've had for a while."

"What do you think I look like, Dunet?" Kreenie bends her head down as mine leans back to look playfully up at her.

I frown. "I think you're playful ... just like a dolphin. And I have always liked your hair!" I hurry frantically. "I just ... cannot figure out what it looks like."

"Have you ever seen a dolphin?" she implores.

"No." I hesitate. "But Liela told me a story!"

"Well," she cackles, placing her hand on her hip, "I will keep playing the part and hope I live up to it!"

"Oh no ..." Lunan leans forward, looking at me with fake fear in his eyes. "What have you done?"

Torie puts her fist in front of her mouth as she tries to control her laughter. "You have awakened the dolphin, Dunet!"

My cheeks feel warm, and I want to bury my face as everyone looks at me and the room breaks out in laughter.

"Stop it, Torie"—Lunan waves his hand up as he hides his face in his arm against the table—"or that will be the death of me!"

I hear a clearing of someone's throat, and jump a little, trying to find the source of the noise.

"Sorry, Marta," Lunan says automatically to an older, white-haired lady seated close to Thomas.

"I was just getting jealous, is all. Carry on." Marta waves her hand.

Torie whispers into Lunan's ear a moment later and Lunan gives a chuckle.

I cock my head at them, feeling a tingle as I lean forward.

A second later, Torie meets my eyes. "Hungry for dessert, Dunet?" I drop my eyes and nod. It is rude to eavesdrop.

"Thomas"—Kreenie clears her throat loudly—"or Chef Feln, as I like to say, made his favorite tonight. Can you guess what it is, Dunet?"

"Chocolate-dipped strawberries?" I pose tentatively.

"Close! Chocolate mousse with succulent raspberry filling," she replies.

My mouth waters at the thought, and I feel relieved that Kreenie has immediately corrected me.

From the other side of the table, Thomas clears his throat casually. "As Kreenie says. She gave that one away."

"As they say, surprises can come from anywhere!" Kreenie beams with self-assurance.

"Or anyone ..." Geon, another older man, mutters humorously from near Thomas. He has graying hair and a clasped jaw that peeks out of a bent face and white-blue eyes.

I startle, looking wide eyed at him. I wonder if he's angry, but seeing the people around him smile, I realize he's not, and I smile in relief.

"Well, I suppose dessert at lunch is fine," Lunan says, leaning back.

"And guess whose idea that was!" Kreenie laces her fingers together under her chin, as she props herself forward on her elbows, legs swinging out beneath her.

I cock my head, not knowing what to say.

Torie blanches for a moment.

"Torie's!"

I attempt to smother a high-pitched squeal at Kreenie's outburst.

Torie shakes it off, smiling warmly at me. "It was all for you, Dunet."

I feel a blush on my cheeks. She really did that for me?

Then Torie speaks, "I think we would consider training you, if not for ..."

My heart leaps, and then drops. "I know. I wish I could, but ..." I say, twisting my hand around my fork.

"You're too young, anyway. I just see a lot in you." Torie says to me with affection.

Does she really? It seems too bright to be true, but ... do I have anything to offer? Or am I just standing here doing nothing? I feel weightless at the praise, but it never quite sinks in. I look away. "That makes me really happy!"

I jump in Kreenie's lap, but I don't feel the joy I put on display at the moment. More and more, I get the feeling of the sunbeams slipping away from my fingers; I wonder what is genuine, and what is me reaching out, for whatever reason, to get that same reaction. I just want them to be happy...

I want everyone to be happy ...

To see that depthless sparkle in their eyes ...

I think.

No—I shake my head, my smile lighting in full. This time it's genuine, like a dazzling light off the water's surface.

I hear a short clap from Thomas several minutes later, then everyone gets up, ready to resume their work again.

Kreenie gets up with me in her arms, spinning me around, before setting me back down in my seat. She extends her hand in a dazzling show. "Time to go!" And I take it, letting her pull me up in a joyous flurry of movement.

I like her so, so much. But ... there's something missing. Something that none of them can fill ... Only Liela can do that.

Around the dinner rush, I start feeling like I am scurrying around again, in the way, melding with the background, with nothing to offer, drowned out by everyone's haste. I feel too out of place, and I know I should probably leave. As I try to turn away, I feel a stiffness, still being drawn back, but I know it would make me a burden to be here any longer.

Instead of invading the kitchen again today, I want to go see Eriena. She will cheer me up, and I know she likes to have company.

I cast a searching glance back. I know I would feel bad if I did not let anyone know I was leaving, and I don't want anyone to worry.

I find Thomas and Torie talking together to the side, a little distance from Kreenie and Lunan.

Torie catches my eye and gives me a friendly smile, saying, "Dunet! What is it?"

"Well, I thought it best if I went now. I ... think I would be getting in the way."

"Of course not!" She places her hands on my shoulders. "But I want you to do what you feel you should. Just come back again soon, okay?"

"I will." I nod, with wavering enthusiasm.

"Take care!" She waves.

"Take care! And goodbye, Thomas."

He clasps my hand in both of his. "Take care, Miss Dunet," he says, pleasantly tilting his head to the side. "This was a gift the younger ones wanted me to give you. They know you like Kreenie's hair." I catch a glint in his eye. "But Kreenie said to fashion it as you will."

He removes his hands and I open my palm to a beautiful baby-blue ribbon and another one of a lovely white. I look at Thomas, then to Torie. "Thank you so much! And ... tell the others I said thank you."

"It would be my pleasure, Dunet. Now, off you go." He chuckles.

I turn and bound away, ribbons silky in hand, my mind settling in a twinkle on everyone in the kitchens. I couldn't possibly pull off Kreenie's look, but maybe I can try something different?

I know! I will ask Liela about it! I feel a burning at my heels to ask her.

I weave my way through the now busy entryway of the castle first, out into the rapidly-cooling evening air, the castle and backdrop of the mountains falling into a reddish-orange hue, though it is still significantly light outside.

I push open Eriena's pen door, my feet mushing at the hay. She whinnies at me as I enter.

I respond with a squeak, a crease along my dimples. "It is good to see you too, Eriena!" And I move my hand to pat her mane. "I wish you could have come with me to the kitchens. It's such an exciting place! If only I wasn't so useless." I give a sorrowful pout of my lips. "Whatever I tell you, promise not to tell Liela." I giggle. "You are my secret keeper!"

Eriena eyes me with intelligence and trust.

"Here!" I reach into a pocket in the folds of my nightgown, pulling out a carrot. "I brought this for you!"

I reach out my hand and she nibbles at it.

"Giving presents is so fun!" My toes curl giddily as I watch her.

Eriena nuzzles me and I giggle again, curling up in the hay.

"You know, I probably shouldn't be wearing this out of bed. But, you know, I feel dreamlike wearing it." I put my finger to my chin, adding, "Like in one of Liela's fairytales!" I squelch my feet against the water-soaked dirt and hay. "I am going to ask Liela to ride you again. I hope we can go. You know ..." I reach my arms around her mane, hugging her and whispering in her ear, "I miss you a lot! I promise to visit more often; I am lonely too. But, Liela has important things ... and I have you!"

I hear the swing of the door and the clear tread of boots that could only be Liela's confident stride.

Throwing my arms around Eriena more, my voice spins as I sing, "I love you and I will be back to see you again!"

I spring up, rushing to the pen door and peeking out. Sure enough, it is Liela. I run out, throwing my arms around her. "Sister!"

"There you are, Dunet! Did you have a fun day?"

"I did! I went to the kitchens again, and then I came here!"

"That sounds exciting! Did you make anything?" she coaxes.

"I made bread with Kreenie, and Torie showed me how they order ingredients!" I pull out the ribbons. "And they gave me this! Can you tie it for me, Liela?" I cock my head.

"Of course, Dunet," she says soothingly, lowering herself to my height. "Now, turn around for me."

I do, with a short spin, toes dusting at the dirt.

"Dunet!" Liela scolds; I feel my stomach drop. "Your feet must be freezing!"

"Oh ... I really meant to wear shoes ..." I grip at my arms, pulling inward.

She starts tying the ribbons in my hair. "It is all right. What matters is that you have fun. But, Dunet," she adds warmly, "it's not healthy to go out like that. I want you to grow up a healthy, happy girl."

"But it is so much fun without shoes!" My voice comes out urgently.

"I know, Dunet." As she skims her hand through my finished ponytail, I can sense her smile on me. "But you can have just as much fun with them. I promise."

Turning around to face her, I ask with disbelief, "I can?"

"I know you can, because we will make that fun together." She grasps my hand, standing. "And we can start now." She swings my hand in hers, looking at me with a cradling light from her olive eyes. "You look good in white."

I bring my hand back, letting the ribbon slide between my fingers. Liela chose the pure white one, tied into a simple ponytail. Somehow, I knew she would, and it makes me feel like I am floating.

"Now, Dunet, are you ready to go home?"

My eyes brighten in joy as I hold her hand, and she lets us go, breaking out into a giddy run through the stable doors. Liela's face shows a complete freedom as her feet skim the ground in an agile breeze, her frame lithe, and I feel like I am soaring on silver wings.

More than anything, I feel alive, and there is a tenderness rushing at my heart. I love it more than anything when Liela breaks *truly* free; when we are in step, and all the world is right ...

When I am free and have the most important person in all the world beside me, and only me.

And I let my pure white ribbon flutter in the breeze behind me ... for her.

~ Memory ~

The Person I Want to See

Liela

I find myself heading to the courtyard once more, the early-morning haze settling in scattered sunbeams through the clouds.

Myllia waits for me at the pond, as usual, the sun dappling on her hair. She lies there on her front side, eyes glazed, in the patch of daisies she seems to love. After a few scattered heartbeats, she looks up at me, breaking into that smile that settles my heart. I always find her a welcome change of pace and tone from my daily routine. And ... even my sister.

I move to sit beside her with a growing familiarity, casting my eyes over her. I find that time always seems to sit still with her. While she wears a dress, today of creamy white, I wear my soldier's uniform—an impressionable forest green, with neatly-tucked creases, azure-blue trimming around the collar, wrists, waist, button line, and down the arms, half-sphered silvered buttons, and Claralis' emblem centered over my left breast—my more formal uniform, befitting of a respectable knight.

A welcoming smile eases onto her features and she shifts her weight a breadth in my direction. Her finger twists lightly around the stem of a daisy, smooth and radiant. "Liela, I am surprised you have time for me, given your duties." She looks at me with warm intensity and my heart stirs.

"Oh." I stumble a little, feeling myself clutch at my words. "I suppose I can always make time. I wanted to come here," I say with rising stability, casting my eyes at her with a gentle tranquility, and finding myself enveloped in her cornflower eyes.

"You know ... that makes me happy," she says softly, pinching at her dress.

"I am honestly glad about that. You know, Myllia ... sometimes it's nice having some relief from everything. You were right when you said my station is weighty. It is, and I normally don't mind, but it's still nice spending time with someone outside all that, regardless—even outside my family," I let myself slip out, with a parched tongue. "I never really let myself relax, and it is somewhat nice."

"You do have your sister, though," she reflects.

"True," I say with a fond smile and a misty feeling. "But it is still nice." I sigh. "I worry about her. I hope she has other friends besides me." I would find it hard to come to terms with, if she did not.

Myllia is silent for a moment. "You know, Liela ... I do think she will be fine, if she has you."

"I just ... I wonder what will happen when I am gone, is all ... I have been naïve in that I never really think about it. I just want the best for her ..." But I always wonder if that is really true.

Myllia gives me a sweet smile, but does not press me.

"Myllia, you don't have any siblings, do you?"

"No ..." Her eyes look dazed again, falling past me. "I mostly spend my time alone."

"I have trouble imagining how lonely that must be," I say, not knowing what I would do without my sister.

"Maybe it is, but I would not know. I always loved books. They brought me everything I needed." She drifts off, smiling peacefully. "I do have a childhood friend, Girena. She is much different than you, though you are just as pretty as she is." Myllia's eyelids lower prettily. "You really are," she adds with a bit of a giggle as I cast my eyes away.

I try to find something to bring the conversation away from me, but I feel at a loss.

Myllia seems to sense my discomfort. "Talk to me about your sister again, if you want to."

"I was thinking about getting her a horse," I blurt out, a little offhandedly. "We like to play in the fields, and I thought I would get her one, so we could ride together."

"That sounds thoughtful, and I am sure she will be pleased. You know," her voice turns sheepish, with an air of interest, "I have never ridden a horse."

"Really? I could show you, if you would like."

She shakes her head, a flush to her cheeks. "I do not think I could manage either." Myllia gives a self-deprecating chuckle. "I have ridden in plenty of carriages, though. Not far from Claralis, of course. My parents take me to an estate occasionally—one out in the countryside, but I prefer the courtyards of this castle."

I agree with her on how restful it can be here, my ears lulled by such a sweet song and the brush of the grass. I wonder if she feels isolated in the estate, but I suppose it would be hard being pent-up there regardless. I still find it ludicrous that she never learned how to ride at her age, lady or not. "I think you should try it, though." I lean forward too quickly, even if my words come out in a light breeze.

"Maybe someday." Myllia laughs lightheartedly. She looks out over the pond, the leaves brushing at its surface in delicate patterns. "Do you have a favorite season, Liela? I think they are all rather lovely, but I like spring best. It is pleasant, and the sounds of the birds are rather soothing. The colors of fall are romantic, too." Her voice sends a chill across my skin.

"I think my favorite would be summer. I like the sound of insects all around and memories of golden stalks of grass and my sister. The bustle of town reminds me of everything we have here, and everything my father and mother worked to create. It's a sentiment that brings me peace. It feels ... nostalgic. But wintertime is nice too. I suppose ..." I trail off, biting at my lip.

"What is it?" Myllia asks, reaching her hand towards me over the grass, as if to demonstrate that she is here.

I stare, as if through the clouds. "I suppose it reminds me of when me and my mother were still close, when we acted like a family. I remember many times of us around the fire, as the cold whipped at the windows." I close my eyes, savoring the memories. Then, I purse my lips bitterly. "Dunet does not remember it ... and I suppose it is best that way. She cannot tell the difference. I am just glad that Dunet still has

Mother." But no matter how hard I try to suppress it, there's a bite to my words—a void my mother's absence has left in my heart. As much as I fail to acknowledge it, I look up to her almost as much as Father. My voice begins trembling as I talk about her, my throat going dry, and I almost break down in the moment. I feel a bit apologetic at the shift in conversation. "I just felt like talking to you, since you trusted me with your family," I say tentatively, as she looks at me with so much care and compassion.

Myllia reaches over and squeezes my hand, and I feel a bit sour for having shifted the conversation to this burdensome place—I have pushed my troubles onto her.

"It must have been hard seeing someone you love so much disappear from your life. You are ... a wonderful person, Liela, and I am sure she sees that. I think she has her reasons, and I hope one day she will move past them and understand you again. I have a feeling you understand her."

I look down at her hand that feels so warm and kind, gripping mine in comfort. My hand curls around hers, warming her in return. "Thank you, Myllia." I inhale deeply. "I really do love her, but I still cannot help wishing it was different. No matter what, though, I am grateful for those memories, and I am thankful she shows her affection for Dunet, if not for me."

She grips my hand tighter, tears glistening in her eyes. "You are a strong person, Liela." She gives me a touching smile that floods my heart.

My voice catches. "And I think *you* are worth more than you think, Myllia. You can do so much with your kindness." Because it nearly breaks my heart to see the tenderness in her eyes, my heart full at how kind she is.

Myllia gives a flattered laugh. "I hope I can. I wonder if you really have the time to spend with me. Your sister is waiting for you, is she not?" But her hand still grips mine, pressing with a light insistence. And ... I admit that I find a strain in my fingers, when I think about letting her go. The touch of her skin sends goosebumps rippling up along my arm, a familiarity seeming to tug me closer to her. My eyes are drawn to the rosiness of her lips and the playful glow of her cheeks.

"I do, Myllia. I will tell her you said hello. But, Myllia," I say with a steady look into her beautiful eyes, "I don't think you should be so quick to dismiss yourself."

"I know. You're right. Thank you, Liela." She gently parts our hands. The warmth of her touch, as it draws away, leaves a dryness in my mouth. "Will you promise to introduce us one day?"

"Of course, I will."

I rise to my feet with a twinge that pulls at my heart, rooting me to my friend. "I want to see you again, Myllia."

She looks up at me, her hands clasped over her lap. "Have a beautiful day with your sister."

"I will, Myllia." As I walk away from her with calm steps, I look back with a grateful smile. She sinks back onto her front side in the grasses, her chin resting over her pudgy forearms. She looks pretty like that, and I realize how warm

I feel when I am around her. I wish she would not dismiss herself like that, but it's just like her.

A copper leaf blows over the cobbled path. The winds gust at the darkening clouds, a prelude to the start of fall. I remark at how beautiful that leaf looks, as it comes to rest at my feet.

A Bold Heart

Liela

I make my way through the back entrance of the castle, directly out from the barracks, my step seemly and practiced. A tree-lined avenue laid down with pebbles crosses the short expanse, a cool canopy playing shadows over my eyes. A stream flows to one side into a pond of lilies, a gentle murmur at my ears, and I am met by a dense clumping of trees grouped near the entrance and several flower beds. The sky above lingers in a light gray, the gradual shift to fall bringing with it the cold Claralis is known for, and it prickles ever slightly at my fingertips.

The back entrance rises in a slim arch, silver-lined, opening onto the scarlet red carpet of a torch-lit hall, peaking high above my head, thick wooden columns set to either side with spacious gaps, opening to the expansive library, lit with burning hearths and filled floor-to-ceiling with books, skylights set high above. Covered lanterns bob with the students. Several sofas and armchairs sit around the corner fireplaces, between antique mantels. Students lounge in the coolness of the room, scattered tables tucked into nooks and between rows, the walls a welcoming wood and floors a faded maroon.

My eyes light up at the sight of Driena and Darnor sitting at a nook.

I know that I can always study in my office at home, but I find myself coming here more often, and I always hope that Driena and Darnor are here whenever we don't specifically schedule a meeting time.

It does bring a pang to avoid home, but I know that I would find it hard to get anything done with Dunet there. She would find me, and that would fracture me too much, to let her know I did not have time for her, like I was putting her off. At home, I usually keep my study for when she is fast asleep, and unlikely to come to my room.

Part of me longs for some uninterrupted time with Driena and Darnor, even if it is study time. Though, even when I am with them, there is a gnawing sensation forever in the back of my mind, that it's not with Dunet. But, beyond that, I just don't have the time for any of them, considering all my duties. I find my time with the two of them a treasure, even when we are largely silent as we study.

Darnor lounges back in a sofa, forehead creased at his study material. He jots down a few notes.

Driena rests on his left side, in an armchair, elegantly upright, with her legs crossed in front of her, gazing pensively at her book.

She notices me first, pulling her eyes up from the book and smiling in a greeting. "Liela, glad you could make it. Darnor and I got here just a little while ago."

Darnor groans, sitting upright. "Honestly, I would not be so sure about joining us, Liela. I have just *finally* found my motivation."

"Of course, you did, Darnor," I tease.

Driena waves her book in the air. "You know what he means."

I move to the other seat, across from Driena and next to Darnor, sinking into its velvety cushions.

Leaning forward, I prop up my chin, elbow on my knee. "Is Driena helping you all right?"

"Actually, he has been rather quiet." Driena ruffles her eyebrows, a frown cresting her lips.

"I have been quite eager to study today," he admits. "Have you been up to anything, Liela?"

"My studying has picked up, as has the intensity of my training. I am sure yours has too, Driena."

She inclines her head at that.

"I thought I would find you two to study with, for today."

"Actually, Liela ..." Driena uncrosses her legs and slips her voice into a more formal flow, "Commander Wheln told me to send you to him when I saw him earlier."

"I hope it is what I think it is," Darnor adds.

Driena nods. "So do I. It's just my intuition, but I hope I am right. I know he is looking to you next, Liela."

"Driena got her seal and her promotion," Darnor says with a casual grin.

"Darnor, I told you *later*," Driena hisses.

"I apologize, Driena, but your accomplishments deserve a mention too."

"Well, thank you, Darnor," she cuts in curtly, then softens her voice. "I really appreciate it."

I feel a growing spark for Driena's accomplishment, knowing how hard she has worked. "Congratulations, Driena! You earned it."

"Thank you, Liela. It was actually more nerve wracking than I thought."

"I really believe that." I can feel a rising knot in my throat.

"But you have my best wishes, Liela." Driena smiles. "I told you, we would make it together."

"I know we will, Driena, just like we promised. I apologize; I cannot study with you for now."

"No need." She rests back elegantly, dropping her hands to her book. "We have all the time in the world."

"Good luck, Liela," Darnor says.

"Congratulations." I shift my gaze to him. "And we are still celebrating her later, right Darnor?"

"Right." He chuckles. "She gets the same treatment as you."

"Hey." I roll my eyes. "No assuming anything."

"Oh, right." He lifts his study material and flicks his wrist at me. "Good luck, Liela."

"Same to you and your studying." I turn briskly to go, my heart stuttering as I try to keep my pace, shaking my head on my way out.

This could be anything.

But they both seem very aware that it's something big. My mouth leaps into a grin. So much for surprises.

Instead of heading out towards the barracks, I turn up the open-air staircase in the lofty hallway, looking down at the scarlet carpeting, then up at the huge, dangling crystal chandeliers glimmering from the ceiling. The staircase is set in polished wood siding with evenly spaced and equally polished wooden knobs along the railing, the steps carpeted in deep forest green, while towering azure blue banners are draped as their compliment along the wall.

The steps lead to a landing, turning left into a section of the castle that protrudes farther from the back, to overhang and wrap around the rear entrance.

Commander Wheln's office is situated behind a short, stylized wall overlooking the expansive library entry area, made private by a door of a simple and polished burgundy with a muted copper knob.

I give a formal rap of my knuckles, twice against the door, and hear Commander Wheln's gruff yet easy voice carry with an authoritative, "Come in."

He looks up from his desk to face me with a memorable formality, crisp and firm. "Cordre." His eyes are a wise agate blue, skin lightly tanned, but close to fair, the lines of his face plain with creases around the edges. His hair is nearly shoulder length, a dark golden blonde, while his hands rest properly on the desk, with a taut, practiced stiffness to them. He wears a suit that looks more in line with a uniform, azure blue, with dark green and white trim, and faded gold buttons.

The wood of his office is antique, creaking slightly at my footfalls; the ceiling hangs low, and his desk is halfway between the short expanse from the door to the window, free from clutter. The window sits in a large circle with a cross of wooden framing meeting in the center, behind the desk, falling on the image of the barracks only a short distance below, behind Commander Wheln's back.

"Commander Wheln," I say, rigid and sure as I stand, awaiting any orders with respectful patience.

I look up to and respect Commander Wheln a great deal—I feel grounded, and nearly reverent in his presence, which has guided me for so long. He has been my mentor for years, and I am, in a way, his prodigy. I am also one of his star students, though that came with much work and sacrifice on my own part. I know him to be honorable, and I don't treat his commitment to me lightly. I want to make him proud and be someone deserving to have his title one day.

"You may sit, Liela," he says with a calm, intent voice, motioning his hand to the chair opposite him, and then setting it back on the desk.

"Of course, Commander." I bow my head in deference and slide into the chair, sitting straight with my hands folded in front of me. I meet his eyes with clarity.

"I surmise from your posture that Tollus gave you a hint of why you're here," Wheln remarks casually. Tollus— Driena Laurel Tollus.

"I don't want to assume, I just know that it is something important," I say with honesty. My voice holds steady, making sure not to let anything else slip.

"As I expected. Cordre." He gives a weighted pause. "After my due consideration, I have decided that my time here has reached its end. As one of several candidates to succeed me, you have my approval. As it stands, you rank the highest in the talent and intellect necessary to lead." He pulls a forest green envelope with a golden seal gracefully from his pocket, and hands it over the table, letting it rest a hand's width from me. "And you have shown more commitment than any, which I truly admire." He gives me a few seconds to let it all sink in, then joins his fingers in a modest appeal. "Should you accept, the command of this city passes to you. I can think of no one more suitable. Congratulations." He dips his head, this time to pay respect to me and my accomplishments. "You have surpassed all my expectations."

"Commander ..." I feel an insurmountable gratitude to my mentor, and exhilaration rushes through my veins. "I feel more honored than I can put into words. And—" I pause, knowing that I can in no way replace him, even with his faith in me. "I accept your offer, and will strive to work with the same commitment to my people and my rank that you have seen in me. I can think of no better way of repaying you."

He leans back, eyes softening in contemplation. "I know you will do well, Liela. You have my faith." I can see kindness in his eyes. "And I trust you not to be too modest with your accomplishments."

"Of course, but I think it's only expected that I should be modest, Commander."

"You no longer answer to me." He smiles with a gracious ease. "I advise you to keep that in mind. You have everything that you need to move forward on your own."

I feel a bit odd, surreal even. It has not really sunk in, and I don't expect it to anytime soon. The man sitting before me answers to *me* now, the words that once came from him will now come from me. Henceforth, I will look within myself for my own strength. He will be retired. But I know I can trust my own judgment, and I will be confident in it, because I dedicated my life to this. I am more than ready; this I know above all else.

I find Driena and Darnor again. Both grin at me, and I still find myself feeling weightless from my promotion. "My ceremony is in a week," I say, donning a mock smug grin. I tell myself it's fake for now, and let myself do it.

"I figured as much. To the star pupil, Liela!" Darnor raises his hand as if he is holding a glass.

"To Liela." Driena rolls her eyes, but copies Darnor anyway. "Honestly, I never doubted you for a second. I can tell by now when Commander Wheln makes a big decision like this."

"Well, Driena" I raise my eyebrows—"you are my second."

"Obviously, I agreed beforehand. But yes, Liela." Her eyes shine at me. "Your will is my command."

I shake my head. "Or we work together—I know you read my thoughts better than I can."

"She can be a little dense," Darnor mutters.

Crossing my arms, I respond surely with, "Not when it matters. I say, in terms of denseness, you are more so."

"Point taken." He sinks back in his chair.

I sink into my chair as well, groaning to dissipate my tension. "Regardless, Driena, I find myself more nervous than I thought I would be. So it helps that you will be there."

"Every step."

I turn to pull my book back out.

"Are you still studying with us?" Darnor eyes me. "No fancy relaxation to celebrate your accomplishments?"

I shake my head. "You know I cannot think like that. I need to keep up my studies. Though, it is true that Commander Wheln offered me an official exemption during the coming week."

"Honestly." Driena shakes her head with a disapproving look. "You work too hard for your own good, Liela."

"I most likely do, but it is what keeps me going." My dreams ... that I would dedicate my entire life to. Without them, I suppose I have nothing.

Driena gives me another meaningful look, before turning back to her book. Darnor does the same. I smile at them—same old friends. I am lucky that I don't really have to leave them with my promotion. At least, Driena will be at my side. I know I could cope without her, but it relieves something within me, to have someone to lean on.

I walk up the stairs to my family's suite, breathing in.

After all this time, it is almost overwhelming to tell my family. I do my best to steady my hands and settle my breath.

At the door of our suite, I take a deep breath and turn the handle, but I know that I am more excited than anything to see father's warm glow and Dunet—with her sparkling energy and bulbous eyes—the one I want to protect the most. And, hopefully, I'll see something from Mother ...

Although, I don't know what to expect or what I even hope for from her. But maybe, just maybe, she will see something in me, and maybe she will understand why I strived so far for so long?

Because I honestly shudder to think of anything else. I know that, if she could just see me, maybe everything would be right again with us. It's naïve and far too simple, magical even ... but it's a small hope, however unreasonable that it is.

I click open the door and step into the hall, a smile appearing on my face. I can hear the clinking from the kitchen, and I know that I am not too late to join them for dinner. I find it a relief that, while not everything is perfect, I do still love dinners with my family, like beautiful memories that still exist in the present, even if they have become tainted compared to my older memories that I hold dear. As much as I love my present, my past was even fonder. I never really dwell on it though, and I could not ask for anything better, outside my mother.

Like this, I know I am truly happy, my chest always so light with each passing day, knowing my heart is at ease and at peace.

I hear a rush of light footfalls and catch Dunet's agile figure a moment later, running towards me. "Sister!" she shrieks in glee, her small lungs puffing from her burst of exertion. "We just finished making dinner!" She glances down, touching her pointer fingers together at the tips. "I thought you might not come."

"Of course, I would, Dunet! There's no need to worry," I say soothingly. "Now, are you ready?"

She looks back up, turning quickly, then skipping away. "You will love it! Mommy helped me tonight, and daddy helped too!"

Oh … My steps falter for a moment. "I cannot wait, Dunet." I pick up my step to follow her, tugging on a smile.

I cross the living room with her, the sun just setting this late evening, through the floor-to-ceiling windows, pale red over the horizon. The silhouettes of the Kalltarris Mountains are set in a light dusting of snow under the brightening stars, across the expanse of the Kallet Plains.

My eyes linger on Mother as I enter the dining room. She gives me a courteous, tight-lipped smile. I return my own.

"Liela!" Father winks at me. "Home later than expected."

"I was held up with something important." I tilt my words as calmly as I can, through my building excitement.

He raises an eyebrow. "I hardly know what to expect."

I breathe in, bringing my heart to a rest. "You might as well sit. The news is a bit ... big." I cannot help my stupid grin.

Father settles down, and Mother's eyes tilt up mildly. Dunet runs over to her chair, squirming on the edge of her seat. It makes me smile and helps reduce my tension.

I breathe out, closing my eyes. "I got promoted." My voice swells in confidence. "To Commander of Claralis." I put a dramatic emphasis on it, leaning into a flourished bow, right arm outstretched, to show off to Dunet and Father. I feel a small squirm, especially with Mother there, but I almost don't care. At times, I can deign to theatrics. I think Father brings it out, and I save it for the best moments. I do feel a bit childlike, even so.

Dunet lets out a small gasp, and I crack my eyes open.

I can see Father with an impressed, admiring look, proud and gentle, a luminous touch to his eyes.

"Well," he says, "I could have sworn I knew this day would come."

Once a look of comprehension forms on her face, Dunet looks from me to Father, and father gives her an encouraging nod. She kicks her chair back clumsily, running over to me, and I stand back, putting my chair a healthy distance behind me as she throws her arms around me. "I knew you could do it, Liela!"

I look up from Dunet to find Mother's wide-eyed look; her lips are pursed, as if in thought. She gives me a short smile, her posture remaining just the same as before, failing to give away much of her reaction.

I let myself gloss over it and bathe in the moment, as I hug Dunet back. Father joins us after a moment, and I can feel the warmth from them both.

And I just feel such an incomprehensible bursting from my heart, up into the clouds.

Then, I catch my mother's eyes again, and it stirs at my heart to see her look ... hesitant, almost. Her hands spread tensely over the table, her back seeming half-inclined to stand and come over to us. It stirs tenderly at my chest, but I cannot ask her to. I acknowledge that this probably does feel awkward for her. I almost feel sympathy.

I nod just slightly, and I hope that she understands that I don't blame her in this moment, before my eyes close once more. Feeling the reassuring warmth of Dunet and Father, I know that they will always be there to guide me and give me strength.

Time That Flows

Dunet

I know I should be happy for how far Liela has come.

I really do ...

But I cannot help feeling a pang at all of it, and a drop in my stomach. With every step, I know she will be further away ... More and more, I have been realizing that.

And I know that it's a selfish thought, but I keep wondering, what happens to me then? It jabs at me like a thorn.

These are thoughts that I know are wrong to feel, but I do feel them.

Everything always seemed so far off ... so inconsequential, that I thought they would never come.

But I knew that, without a doubt, Liela would become Commander, because that is who she is. And I was right, as much as I dreaded it somewhere at the back of my mind. The sister I know is dedicated beyond compare ... beyond dreams.

And I feel like I am in her shadow. I am starting to look around, realizing that I don't know what to do.

I want to ignore this for as long as possible ... because these thoughts act as a swirling haze across my eyes, blinding me.

I don't know where to look.

When I was born, I had a choice. It passed my ears over the years, ever-present, but so distant and muffled. Liela would hold my hand through those whispers, spinning me beautiful fantasies and singing me ethereal lullabies.

She still is holding my hand, and she still whispers to me and sings, but I could always tell that something was on the horizon for her that was much bigger than me.

She reaches for it, as if she is reaching for me.

I always found her wish fuzzy and blinding, as much as I was mesmerized by it. What good does protecting someone do, if she must be away for so long just to complete that wish?

What is she protecting me from, anyway?

And why must I choose?

I never understood why it had to be me, or her.

My choice is to rule Claralis, or to let Liela rule for me. Either way, she will lead Claralis' armies.

But if I choose not to rule, then she does ... and I push everything onto her.

She is a selfless person, and I know it would be unfair to her.

I am beginning to understand that she is starting to crack at the edges from the strain, even as we play. It mirrors in her eyes.

I think she thinks I cannot see it, and I probably hardly understand beyond my narrow grasp of her blazing image.

But ... I feel cold at the presentation of my rule.

I want Liela to rule in my place; I clutch my hands to my chest, my eyes squeezing shut with the prickle of tears. I want her to. Yet, my wish seems to grate against my ears.

Is that so terrible?

But ... I should have no reason to think that way.

Liela told me helping people was good.

She also said that no one would blame me if I did not want to rule.

And yet, I feel such a weight pressing at my chest, suffocating me ...

It still feels far off, but every day it presses closer.

I have nothing to give anyone and everything to give Liela.

She needs me ... so I want to be with her.

I make her smile ... so I reach out to her.

I cling to her because she loves me ...

And I love her ...

But I guess not enough ... to avoid pushing something else onto her.

I swing my legs out behind me, fluffing my clenched hands against the pillow repeatedly.

I feel an emptiness in my chest.

I just want her to be with me, but she cannot play by my side while she is gone.

So, I wait for her to come back … every day.

I wait to see her smile and my sparkling reflection in her eyes.

It warms my cheeks to make her happy.

It makes me feel …

I scrunch my face up, squeezing Ceilia against my chest.

Good about myself—an ease in my chest when I know I am needed …

Maybe I should stop moping in bed?

I know Liela would not want me to do that, and I never want her to see me in this spiraling cold, with the walls of my mind pressing in on me.

Rolling over, I gaze at the spiraling doves, stars, and flowers painted over my head, my mouth forming a smile.

I feel a tingling rush once more, then I jump out of bed.

Remembering Liela's disapproval of me not wearing shoes, I pull a pair on- sunny yellow slip-ons, comfy and warm. I don't have many pairs, because I have never liked wearing them.

Liela would scold me for it, and mommy and daddy would insist on me wearing shoes, but there was always a wonder and lightness I found without them.

I glance at my closet, pouting, and decide that I don't particularly want to wear anything besides a nightgown—this one is a pink-red, strawberry color with white lace.

Just in case, I snatch my honey-colored satchel, which Liela got me, because it matched my hair. I throw in the mini jars from my paint collection, listening to the little jingle they make that gives me a fuzzy feeling, and I also grab my art pad, in case I have nothing to do. I sometimes like going to the gardens or the meadow, to paint and let my mind wander. Liela, mom, and dad all have their own collections of my artwork, and it gives me a fluffy feeling to see them displayed. I give my best paintings to Liela; she always says she loves them. Even if it was a lie, I would still soak up that praise, because it would be from her—my best friend, my idol ... and the person who needs me.

My lips wobble.

I realized that that was part of why I cling to her ...

Pushing through this painful realization, I finish stuffing my supplies into my satchel.

I will be a ray of sunshine for Liela, and for everyone.

I beam, because that is who I am.

I twirl in front of my mirror, staring at the image Liela loves: the dimples on my rosy cheeks, and my soft features, my shining, fair skin, sapphire eyes so intensely bright, and this grin I wear, pasted on as if by sunshine. Pressing my palms to my cheeks, I squint and giggle.

Swiveling on one foot, while the other splays out straight at an angle, and then lands with merry mischief in the direction of the door, I turn to leave.

I wonder what to do ...

In two hours, I will have lessons with Halfern. I feel an itch across my skin. I like Halfern and his gentle, slow teaching, but I find everything so much, spiraling far up and out of my reach. My mind seems to wander half the time, but I understand my lessons are important, and I want to make my family proud.

I ... couldn't bear them being disappointed in me. The possibility twists frightfully at my chest, as it drops into oblivion.

Halfern seems content enough, but I wonder if he is disappointed with me.

I wonder whether or not he *should* be.

I shake my head, giddily chasing out all the thoughts I don't know how to deal with, and then I skip out of the room, mouth naturally forming a smile.

Because I do very much feel carefree, despite the looming pressures that I cannot help cocking my head and scrunching my face at.

I twist around the doorframe, my hand clinging to the wall and my body swiveling into the hallway.

For a moment, I feel magical. It is a passing moment, because I am alone, but I still close my eyes to savor it.

I open them again.

I want to go to the kitchens. It's the place I love most in the castle, aside from my home and the gardens and the fields Liela and I play in.

I know they're older than me, but Torie, Kreenie, Lunan, and everyone there are like best friends. Maybe, not exactly ... they do treat me like a child.

But they never mind me there.

I know what to do, and what makes them smile.

I dash down the stairs, white trailing behind fluttering strawberry. I skim my hand over the wall, feeling the rush of everything. I like these stairs. They're small and close, like an enchanting gateway, and I just love the spiral!

I skid through the open entryway and find myself in the kitchens.

I feel adrift, standing there alone, my eyes searching without a clear goal in mind, but that all disappears as I see Kreenie enthusiastically waving at me from across the room. Then, she bounds over to me.

"Dunet! It's amazing to see you!"

"Hi, Kreenie! Can I help you today?" I ask.

"Hm ..." She frowns, plucking at her left pigtail. "About that: Torie has an exam today. She wants you rooting for her, but ... well ..." She looks away. "I could play with you."

My heart catches, and I move my hands behind my back, to hide their shaking. She seems off, and it jabs at me harshly.

Kreenie looks at me again. "It has nothing to do with you." She looks serious, for once ... This isn't the playful bubbliness I know.

Holding my lip, so it does not quiver, I nod, then turn away. "No, it's fine! Sorry, Kreenie. Tell her good luck!" But my voice screeches in my ears.

She runs after me, falling into step and swinging her arms by her sides. "Want to go outside?"

"Yes, please!" I nod, though my heart trembles from disappointing her. "Are ... your studies going well too?" My question feels fake, leaving my lips dryly.

"Oh, perfect!" she chimes, then pulls at my wrist. Our walk turns into a skip, and I watch her pigtails bouncing out of the corner of my eye. "Run with me, Dunet!"

I pick up the pace and we explode into one of the courtyards, but I cannot help feeling an icy uncertainty. "Kreenie," I press her, "why did you come with me?"

She twirls my arm, spinning me. I let a giggle slide off my numb lips. "Because I wanted to be with you!"

My face neutralizes again all too quickly, vigor disappearing into pallid cheeks. "But what about Torie?"

"I told her my support will reach across the sun and stars to her ... but I wanted to do something for her." She sticks out her tongue, pressing her palm to her chest. "The love for the people I care about is eternal, and that includes both you and Torie. She will be just fine! I think I am a bit of an annoyance ... in all the best ways."

"For her?" I ask in a weak voice.

"Yes!" She pokes my cheek. "Though I don't know how to go about it. Torie is horribly cruel, you know," she chides with a lack of conviction. "And Thomas too ... He cares about you, you know?" Kreenie furiously pulls at her pigtails, then pauses, eyeing me. "You know, I always wondered what you would look like with pigtails." She stops pulling her hair. "Anyway, off topic, but they're both worried and I don't know what to do. Well, not 'worried' exactly, but I think they worry. Not that I mind at all! I love adventures! Anyway, Torie started to notice that you looked down, and I guess she had a talk with someone. Well ... I did promise not to tell you anything, so I can't tell you much else. Whoops!" She bends forward inquisitively. "So, what do you say we find one? Until Torie finishes, and then we can tell them all the fun we had?"

My heart drops even lower than it was before. They ... don't want me?

"Anyway, find new friends, Dunet! Um ... I think that was all ..." She searches me with her eyes. "Torie ... thought I should be the one to talk to you. Just a quick talk, she said, and then everything can go back to normal!" She grins. "You know?"

"I don't want to stop coming here." I find it hard to meet her eyes.

"Of course not! Hey!" She grabs my hand. "It's all right. Everything is just fine, and we are all still here." She looks

Caroline Sophia Hamel

around. "Let us go find something! See all those leaves falling, or I could teach you how to swim like a butterfly!"

I giggle. "How does that work?"

"We could find out! Come on, Dunet!" She grabs my hand, pulling me along. "Want me to give you a piggyback?"

"Can we?" I climb onto her back, hiding my eyes that rapidly start to sting.

"But, Dunet ... I may not be good at this, but I want to keep my promise. Will you find some new friends for me? Torie thinks you look ... well, it may have confused me, but I think I get it ..."

"Yes," I lie. I know that, despite appearing happy and joyous, it is like no one can relate to me and I am in a dark, empty pit ... like no one can see me as someone to be their friend. I don't ... know how to have friends.

And everyone thinks I am fine, and eternally happy. Until now.

I want desperately to keep this all contained, this feeling of being alone, as just a shadow within me.

That is how I want them to see me, but sometimes I feel so tired ...

Like my heart is dragging ...

And Kreenie, Torie, Thomas ... they all scare me now ...

I just want Liela back.

I want to curl up in her arms as she reads to me.

But I pull on a smile and give into my delusions: that everything is just fine.

Kreenie stayed with me. Somehow, that matters.

I don't know why she would, and I know I should not keep her like this.

But I pull the smile to my face and play along, raising my head and pointing over her shoulder at the falling crisps of leaves, beautiful in their reds and oranges ... and the yellow ones gleam like the sun.

They still fall so softly, bringing my world back into a gentle, whirling lull ...

Contentment of Sunbeams

Liela

My eyes fall over the crest of the arch forming the courtyard, and I breathe in deeply. Then, passing under the arch, my steps light at the prospect of seeing her. It has been far too long. Perhaps not long at all, but I miss her already.

Whenever I have a break from my duties, studying, Dunet, Driena, and Darnor, I come here. Sometimes between everything, because I know those moments are fleeting.

With her, I can give everything, and it feels so soft in my chest. My eyes flicker to the lovely wonder of the courtyard.

I scan the clearing, my heart dropping for a moment when I don't see her. I release a sigh, ready to turn back, before I notice her, and my heart skips a beat, my skin tingling with goosebumps.

She is by the pond, as she usually is, under the sagging boughs of the tree, amid a patch of daisies, daffodils, and the light greens of the grasses, the early traces of fall sketching coppery leaves over the water's edge, the winds rippling lightly at the grasses and skimming playfully at the whites of her ankles in tan, rib-caged sandals, highlighting the soft arch of her foot and her smooth, pudgy legs.

The water laps at her feet as she rests there, her arms wrapped around her knees, looking distantly over the still water. I find myself drawn to that look, so far off and dreamy. It makes her look ethereal, in this little courtyard. I find it curious how she can delve so far into whatever world she is imagining, but I know from her face that it is a deep longing of hers.

As I approach her, she looks up, smiling warmly at me like a spring blossom; she wears another dress, this one light pink, with white frills, the edges gracing her bare shoulders and ankles, like rippled water over glass. She looks very pretty in it. Her hair is curled, springy almost.

"Myllia." I look at her with a stirring fondness, my breath catching ever so slightly. "You look well." Dazzling, to be honest—I have never had a friend catch my eye like she can. But more than that, her heart is beautiful, and that is what truly catches me.

"Liela!" And I can hear a note like a song in her voice, as she turns to face me, hands scrunching daintily in her lap, after she first absentmindedly twirls her finger through a curl of her hair and places it behind one of her fair ears. "I was hoping you would come. I love this weather too." She sits in the remaining summer sun, which is slightly dimmer in the approaching fall, the scattering leaves around her. The sun falls on her in splotches of color, through the tree above.

"Of course, I would, Myllia," I say, treasuring the sight of her. "And," I say lightly, "I think it is nice, too."

I move to sit down next to her, and she rests her head back against the grass, closing her eyes. "Have you ever stopped to feel the grass, Liela?" She looks up at me with a sparkle of whimsy, her voice as sweet as always. A soft breeze blows over the water, which ripples peacefully in front of us.

I laugh. "Not that I can think of."

"But you know, Liela." Myllia sighs. "Sometimes I wonder what I am doing with my life. This is all nice and it takes my mind off things ... but when I think about it, I realize I really am doing nothing with my time." She looks out, her eyes drifting, but still lovely, even as she tugs at my heart.

"Myllia," I say with a gentle drop of my voice, "I know that you will find something that will make you happy, and that you can strive for. I think you have everything that you need."

Her face relaxes. "Maybe I do?" Her voice grows distant, and I swallow thickly, wanting to reach out. "My parents are trying to court me to a lord's son. I thought I should let you know, since ..." She closes her. "Well, maybe you don't realize it, Liela, but you are starting to mean a lot to me."

I stay silent, but feel a delicate flutter through my chest at her words, even if everything else sinks in and I desperately want to reach across that gap and comfort her. I reach over and touch her hand, to which she takes a breath. My own hand freezes on hers as an unexplainable bliss races through my fingertips.

"Maybe I do not want it, but I find myself wanting to make them happy." She gives a pause, her eyes meeting the grass. "I like having time to myself. My parents ... Well, I do not see them a lot." She glances at me with a sweet smile, like she is telling me not to bother—that she does not mind.

My mouth feels a little bit dry, for some reason. "I am sorry about that, Myllia. I think that you should be with whoever you want."

"I think so too." She giggles abruptly, before her eyes turn heartbreakingly sullen again, like they are crying out to me. "But, really … I think this is something I need to figure out for myself." She stares distantly up at the sky. "I just wanted you to know."

"Thank you, Myllia. You know, I wish you the best," I lay out in compassion, even if a painful, confusing longing claws at my chest.

"I know you do, Liela, and maybe I should start taking more initiative, but … I hate to come off as dour."

"It is okay, Myllia, really."

"I knew you would say that, but still." She sighs again, closing her eyes. "You know, Liela …" She smiles at me with such tenderness, her eyes opening on me again with a shine. "I have been coming here a lot more."

"Really?" I stumble.

"I think this is my favorite place now."

I give a content smile, my eyes not leaving hers as I take in the soft greens behind her curls. "I am happy about that, Myllia."

"I hoped you would be." Her cornflower eyes glint sweetly.

"It is rather nice." I shift my gaze away, back to the pond, but I find that doing so is nearly painful.

"That is not all I was talking about." I swear, she flits her eyelashes at me.

I blink, in a daze.

She giggles again, a hand to her mouth. "You know, I always find it surreal how you take your position and your life. It seems rather stressful."

My mind is soothed by the allure of her giggle and her words, and I feel a strong urge to look away, even though my eyes wish to cling to her. "Maybe it should be. I know it is a lot to live up to, but I have always been happy for it."

"You always sound like you have a lot of confidence, Liela. You know, I admire that about you."

"Well, I have a reason to be confident. I think you will find that, Myllia," I say steadily.

Dreamily, she looks me over.

I feel hot all of a sudden, and I shift a little. "What is it?"

"Oh, I just thought you looked pretty," she murmurs.

I laugh. Somehow, her words lift a weight off me, even if my skin burns with a sudden flair and my heart picks up.

"Your uniform looks good on you. Green really does suit you."

It is becoming difficult to meet her dazzling eyes. "It's my favorite color—deep green."

"That sounds like you," Myllia replies knowingly. Is she teasing me?

"And yours?" I try drawing attention away from myself, but I genuinely want to know.

"Yellow. It is bright and cheerful."

My mind lights on a memory that brings a nostalgic smile to my face. "That is the color you were wearing when I met you."

"Yes," Myllia replies, her eyes trailing me longingly.

That memory brings a thrill to my heart. "Myllia ..." I pause for a moment, suddenly brought out of my daze and into the present. "I have a ceremony coming up and ... I was wondering if you would come." I look at her, my breath catching as my heart beats more wildly than it should.

Her face brightens. "Of course, I will!" She grasps my hands. "I would love to, Liela!"

A surge of relief puts me at ease, making it so I can breathe calmly again. "I thought it would settle my mind some, to know that you would be there." And it does—I had been wanting to ask her to come. This is ... a bit of a surreal experience, but a very important event for me, and a steppingstone towards my future ... and as someone who is important to me, I want Myllia there, as much as I want Dunet there.

And, I admit, a part of me wants her there more ...

I am doing this all for Dunet, but I cannot help feeling that it's somehow special to have Myllia there. Because it means something different to me ... to have someone who gives me a different, indescribable joy, but also a soft, grounding touch, and a way to share and express myself that I just cannot, or maybe *don't want*, with Dunet.

She looks down with a glossy sheen to her eyes. "I am happy that you would invite me, Liela."

My heart jumps, but I ease its racing. "Of course. I really want you to be there. It's the ceremony for me to become commander, in five days."

Her breath catches beautifully. "Liela, I am so happy for you!"

I feel a flutter at that. This is a moment that is so important to me—a moment I have been waiting for and working towards. "Myllia." I lie back in the grass, closing my eyes and letting myself feel its softness this time. "Sometimes I wish I could just stay here with you."

I don't hear anything for a moment, except the soft rustling of the wind, and then the gentle brush of fabric close by my ear.

"You're right, Myllia. It feels so peaceful." I open my eyes to see the dazzling image of her only a breath away.

She gives a tiny smile, her arms clutched furtively over her chest, fingers carefully gripped over her elbows, a subtle tension in her body.

I do long to stay, but ... not today. "I am sorry, Myllia, but I better be going."

"I know." She closes her eyes. "I knew you would say that."

I feel a tearing at my heart.

"But you should not worry, Liela. You know, I cannot wait for you to fulfill your dream. And I promise"—I hear a shiver in her voice—"I will be the best version of myself, for you. I just ..." She stops with a tremble, going silent. "Just wait for me, Liela ..." She trails off, opening her eyes again. "You should go."

I hesitate. My voice comes out adrift. "I may be busier in the coming days, Myllia ... but ..." I lace my words with as much meaning and care as I can. "I still want to make time for you. As much as I can."

She looks up at me, her eyes fluttering dreamily as her dress plays in the wind over the fatness of her frame. "And I will be here waiting for you."

I turn to go. When I do, I cast one last look back, finding her eyes still gazing at me ...

And I am torn to look away ...

But I do, and I smile; my heart soars even as it pains me to leave.

A Strained Smile

Dunet

I peer into the room, tense hands gripped tightly behind my back. I glance through the tower room, as if through a tunnel. It looks darker than it should, but I put a spring into my step and layer a shine on my eyes, plastering a sunny smile on my face that twitches into full dimples.

This is my classroom, besides my tutoring with Halfern. A breeze-filled room, the shimmering white curtains rustling in early autumn. The classroom takes up half of one of the larger towers. Oaken desks cover the bright coppers of the rugs and the shining white walls of marble, one of the few imports in the castle. The other children here are all close to my age, daughters or sons of lords.

I glance around again, pretending to be turning my head in curiosity.

I can see Grace, Autumn, Silvia, and Lena chattering with a sunny buzz around the center of the room, ribbons, and late summer dresses, all with pleasant, well-kept faces. Loreen and Shila sit back in a corner, hair braided in their nook by the window. Connor sits alone, farthest from anyone else, and he meets my eyes with deep turquoise ones, before quickly snapping them away. James, Elliot, and Julia sit perched on desks, their legs swinging. Shane, Tella, and Auna sit in soft conversation, crisscrossed on the rugs. I notice Lily, a girl with seawater blue eyes, straight bangs nearly to her eyebrows, a plain brown dress, and braided blonde pigtails, underneath a sunhat, tilt her gaze up to me from over her book. Then, she quickly turns down and bites her lip.

I ruffle my head, skipping over to the nearest group.

"Hi!" I flitter in a high pitch to Grace, Autumn, Silvia, and Lena.

They glance up, and Grace, with her blonde-plaited hair, honey eyes, and full, refined face, beams with a, "Hi, Dunet!"

I cock my head. "How have you been?"

"Splendid, Dunet," she says with a sweet, distant smile. "And you?"

"Oh, wonderful!" I spurt.

"That is so *good*, Dunet!" Her smile blooms with ease. "I am glad you feel that way."

"Grace," Lena murmurs with a giggle. She has bright blue eyes, clear skin, and brunette hair fixed in a bob.

"Hmm ..." Grace turns away with a parsing of her lips. "What was that, Lena?"

My breath picks up as their words mix in my ears.

"Anyway, was there something you wanted to talk about, Dunet?"

I shake my head, feeling far away. "No, not really."

"Oh, well." She starts turning away, her smile absent again, but bright when I was there, and I craved it, "It was nice to talk to you."

I dig my nails into my skin as I grip my wrist harshly. "You too!"

I ease my grip slowly off my wrist as I turn away, skipping again and trying not to scurry.

I go over to Auna, Shane, and Tella, who brighten upon seeing me. "Dunet, sit with us!" Auna says, with her flaming copper hair, freckled face, and golden-brown eyes, exuding warmth.

Shane nods at me, with his straw-yellow hair and faded freckles.

Tella, platinum blonde hair in a single braid with a bright-green bow tied at the end, gentle, crystal-blue eyes, and an angular face, nods at me and says in wispy voice, "Hello, Dunet."

"Hi!" I settle down, then lean forward. "How are you?"

Shane grins with unsteady lips. "Swell, I think. We were just talking about our recent trip to the market."

"It was wonderful!" Auna says.

Tella nods along. "I cannot remember how many things we even did."

Auna leans forward and my mind goes blank. "So?"

"Oh ... I have been ... good lately ..." I trail.

"Anything fun?"

"I was waiting to play with my sister!"

"Oh, that sounds fun!"

"My sister would not do that," Tella titters. "Dunet, what would you rather smell, honeysuckle or roses?"

"Oh, well, I don't know." I pause again, my mind twisting for an answer.

"No bother," she says, turning back to Shane. "Shane, do you not think your parents could let you go off again with Auna and me?" She cocks her head, eyes bright.

"Oh, maybe ..." he replies.

Again, I start feeling adrift, lost in a swirling vortex of confusion. I never know what to say; my mind gets caught, as I am pushed aside by even the most well-intentioned and kind people. Seeing their smiles makes me feel weightless, if only for a brief moment, but everything is fuzzy after that, even as I try to reach out with a trembling hand and a bright smile.

It seems clear that while they like me ... everyone seems pleasant around me, really ... it feels like there's such a gap that I am not actually there, and I am left behind.

I think people assume I don't mind, but it makes me feel like a lone petal in a vortex, watching the world blur ...

I don't know why everything feels fuzzy. Why I try to catch their eyes and they're there to catch mine if only for a fleeting moment, but it only throws me further away.

I know that there must be something wrong with me.

Sun-Kissed Petals

Dunet

I dart through the waving fields of grass, laughing in delight as I skim the tips of my fingers past the coarse, golden stalks. The wind ripples over them, bending the stalks and tossing my hair over my face. The air kisses me in the warmth of the sun, not quite the cool of fall. But they still shimmer like a golden ocean, on the precipice of an eternal frost crackling at their stems.

Liela lightly tackles me, and I start rolling with a gleeful shriek down the slight incline, parting the grasses as I go. She runs after me and I let loose another giddy shriek, lifting my head out of the flattened stalks.

"Dunet!" Liela laughs, her hands lax at her sides, face at ease. "You're going to ruin your dress!" She slows down to a walk next to my burrowed form. "Quite the little princess." She smiles down at me, eyes stirring with fondness. Her hair is tied back, and she wears red-brown riding pants, with a matching shirt, silver belt and forest green and black coat, and gray riding boots.

I giggle at her comment. "And you look like a prince!"

"Commander of Claralis, at your service." With that, she gives an extravagant bow from her tall, knightly frame, and then plops down beside me, dark browns of her ponytail trailing on the grasses in thin strands. She reaches up to shield her face with her thin hand, before letting it fall, all the tension gone as her face relaxes and her eyes cast up. We gaze at the clouds crossing the sky, the sun filtering through the stocks of grass like a shimmering golden memory.

I elbow Liela with a giggle, tucking my face into the grass in the opposite direction.

I feel a settling in my chest, and I turn over as Liela stretches out beside me.

I reach up to the clouds with both my hands, grasping at their puffiness, and then I point up at one. "That one looks like Vel!"

Liela gives a hearty laugh. "You're right. And that one looks like Eriena." She points, finger tracing at a cloud.

"I like her!"

She smiles with the affection of a warm hug. "I knew you would. I am sure you two will be good friends."

"We will! We will be the very best of friends!" And I feel all my lofty confidence simmering in that sure face.

Well, *second* best friend. I let my eyes wander over the warming sun and blue sky, the golden stalks waving across my eyelids and bringing me into a drowsy state.

But I want to keep playing. I scramble to my feet in a sudden flurry.

Liela does the same, dusting at her arms as she rises, a glint in her eyes as she seems to prod me.

I give a twirl, diving back into the liquid wall of grasses, brushing the stocks aside in prickly ripples, and I give a shriek of laughter as I hear Liela's fluid steps. My feet lift from the ground in an asymmetrical rhythm and my heart rises with them, as if I can fly into the clouds and become the very wind itself!

A Heart Yearning for a Pure Dove

Liela

I sit beneath the tree, Dunet in my lap and my mind bathed in a surreal, dream-like warmth. The flowers of the courtyard sprawl out around us in yellows, reds, and blues of bright, fairytale shades that dance in the calm, fluttering breeze.

Dunet plucks a blossom with her tiny, dove-white hand as I read to her, her eyes large and shining.

I note it with a small smile, watching her gaze flit from one curiosity to another, even as she glances at me out of the corner of her eye with a warm glow.

My ears catch her stomach growling voraciously, to which she looks at herself with a frown and a hurried glimpse at me, before turning her eyes away again and pressing her fingers to the blossom.

I pause, lowering the book and inquiring, "Are you hungry, Dunet?"

She shakes her head. "I want you to keep reading!"

I smile with a delicate light to my eyes. "I know you do. But you need to eat. It will not do your imagination any good to listen on an empty stomach."

She pauses, her eyes drooping as she shifts off my lap. I reach for a snack—several blueberries and some honey-coated bread. I picked them out just for her.

She kneels in front of me as I hand her the food, and she gobbles them up. I feel a tingling along the corners of my mouth as my mind slips into the softness of a cradled world, one that I always want for her.

She sucks the last traces off her fingers and then stares at me with orb-like, sapphire eyes and glowing, puffy cheeks, the gentle, messy waves of her buttery hair falling onto her shoulders like the angel that she is.

"You want me to read more?"

She nods vigorously. "I do!"

"All right, then." I pick up the book, turning over the pages to the spot where we left off.

Dunet sinks into me, occasionally taking another bite of bread. Her breath settles into a steady pattern.

I finish up the chapter, closing the book with a brush of my hand. Dunet's eyelids droop, and I start to hum to her.

The clouds of dreams,

Clutched on the wind,

Steady and light,

Filled with moonbeams;

Clutched to my breast,

A prayer of light,

And a steady happiness

I wish in the clouds;

The sun will not wash away,

The wind not tear apart,

The rain will not erase this joy of day;

Something of love,

Something of heart,

Something I never want to give away;

For she reaches the sky that I never will,

Caresses the light,

And holds my hand;

An angel of light,

Free as a sprite,

Bright and merry, and a dream of day;

Caroline Sophia Hamel

She holds a flower to all the world,

A flower that must never fade away.

I feel her breath loosen as I finish the song, her small body a gentle weight, as much in sleep as when awake. I look fondly at her. The only sounds I hear are the chirping of the birds that lull at my heart.

Dunet is my fairytale, and I hope she stays forever in one of her own, for it brings me such ease to see her carefree face, unburdened, filled with a never-ending joy.

A Timid Longing

Liela

I sit up from my desk, taken out of the intensity of my thoughts by a delicate knock at the door. I barely hear it as I pour over my work with a crease in my brow—reports and paperwork from the day—even if my formal duties are done. I have felt a lot of pressure lately, but I can deal with it. I am ready for it ... and I would gladly take it all. I just finished a meeting with Commander Wheln, one of many over the last few days. I still don't think I can replace him, but I trust his judgment. He has my utmost respect.

"Come in." I find my voice, after a moment. The light padding of the rain against the window feels like company, and it had started to lull me into a sleepy trance. Not to say that I will not miss summer, but I would rather be pent up inside with this calming sound playing in the background.

When the door opens, my eyes widen at Myllia. I am honestly so used to seeing her in the courtyard that she seems out of place here. I cannot recall her ever visiting me anywhere else.

"Liela ..." She clutches at her rippling plum dress, casting her eyes around the room, before resting them on me and smiling, an alluring twinkle in them. She looks just as stunning here as she would look in any courtyard. Although, I do wish I could see her there instead.

I turn in my seat, my back still straight, but aching. I forget it at this moment though, as my lips pull up irresistibly to see her, and I feel an immediate racing in my heart. I search for another chair, for her to sit. "Myllia, we can talk outside, if you like."

She shakes her head, moving over to the edge of my bed, before shifting back with ease, and folding her hands over her lap, fingers clasped tightly. Her legs cross, feet slipped into beautiful crystal-blue flats. "I just thought I would come to see you. You look tired." Her eyes take me in.

I had not realized that, and I give a faint smile. "I guess I may be just a little busy. And ..." I draw in a breath; there is a small sinking feeling in my heart. "I suppose I haven't come to see you in a while."

"I know you're busy. You do not have to feel sorry about it ... That is why I visited, though, now that you are done for the day. Perhaps I was a little lonely." She unfolds her hands, fiddling with the creases of her dress, as her chest deflates.

I feel curious about that. "Who told you I was done?"

"Darnor. Well, I just met him when I was inquiring about you. He thought you might be."

I am pleased to hear about Darnor—I am very much glad to be on mutual terms with him once more, and to be able to spend so much time with him again. Thinking of Dunet, I realize I have barely seen her these past few days.

Myllia seems to read my expression; her eyes soften. "What is it?"

"I have not spent enough time with my sister recently."

"From what you told me about Dunet, I am sure she will understand." She gives a kind smile.

I shift the conversation, after a brief pause. "How have you been?"

"I have been well. Mostly, at least. My parents still have me studying under that tutor—Leniel is his name. I am rather grateful for it, but they never planned anything important for me. I am still spending much of my free time away, in the courtyard. I tried the north gardens, too. They were rather nice. Maybe I have a bit too much time for someone my age." She sighs, looking out the window. "It is getting late. Perhaps I should go ..."

It had not been that long since she got here, and I wonder at that, feeling a longing in my heart. But I always feel a little more at ease when I see her, even if I feel an emptiness at her leaving again. I smile pleasantly at her. "Good night, Myllia."

"Good night." She closes the door lightly as she leaves, and my eyes catch and linger on her fluttering dress as she does. I turn back to my desk, before deciding to turn in for the night after a moment's hesitation.

A Dream that Burns Brightly

Liela

I take a deep breath, feeling a growing tingling sensation that I try to tame.

Closing my eyes, I breathe. This is it—this is everything that my life has been leading up to.

But it feels so surreal, and my heart beats perilously as I open my eyes to gaze at the silver-twined doors ahead of me, the arc a proud portal of darkened wood.

"Liela," comes Driena's soft, direct voice. I can see her out of the corner of my eye. "You can do this. And, if it helps ..." Her mouth quirks with uncertainty. "I am probably just as nervous." Regardless, she looks so poised and regal there, with azure-blue garments and silver trim. Not quite the same complement to her figure as violet over her dark hair and fair skin, but she still looks as gracefully intelligent as ever, her eyes looking onward with the steady fires of purpose. Her azure decorum is set to complement my forest green of Claralis—deep green jacket, with gold buttons running up the front and set into the shoulders, copper-gold leg armor, polished silver gauntlets, and rustic auburn boots.

"You know, I have been waiting for this moment for years, Driena ..." I turn to her, shaking my head. "Yet I honestly think you are the only thing grounding me in this moment." My voice falls to a prayer. "I just want to make my sister proud."

"You will, Liela, because you know she wants this for you more than anyone." Her voice carries a soothing conviction with her words.

I nod to her, my heart balancing on the precipice of anticipation, the exhilaration of the moment coursing through my veins.

"Are you ready to show off, Liela?"

I roll my eyes. "Like you have anyone to show off to."

She turns her face away, and I swear, I see the flush of her cheeks. "I do this for no one."

I let loose a strained breath that falls into a chuckle. Two attendants in crisp-white tunics move to slowly draw the doors open, to a glimpse of the setting sun, cascading in ribbons of liquid gold.

The massive audience fills the huge amphitheater to the brim. The amphitheater is reserved for spectacles such as this, housing wooden benches with lavish cushions, the walkways set in polished wood, crossing from four sides and meeting at a marble dais in the center. Short-trimmed grass fills in the gaps, and thigh-high, trimmed hedges line the walkways in ceremonial fashion.

I glance out of the corner of my eye to see Dunet leaning forward, and it brings a thrill to my heart to see her there. My family sits in the center of the crowd, halfway up from the ground and to my left, on an ornate balcony protruding from the seating, a forest green and azure blue banner hanging from its front. Father sits to one side in a high-backed chair, placing a hand on her back and conversing with mother, who sits on Dunet's other side, with an intense poise.

Dunet sits up quickly and waves, bringing my thrill even further. It takes all the effort in the world not to wave back.

I reach the end of the walkway, where Commander Wheln stands modestly, his face calm, reassuring, and his hair is neatly combed for the moment. He wears a faded white uniform of retirement. I let go the barest of exhales. This seems unreal, reminding myself that Driena is at my back, I take a step forward, onto the dais.

Commander Wheln looks upon me with a steadying nod. "Liela, heir to your father's throne, you have surpassed the highest honor in rising to the command of Claralis. Do you promise to give your life to the protection of your people?"

I glance slightly in the direction of my family, and then my comrades and friends, my heart lifting at the pride dancing in their eyes, pushing me onward. I try to resist the urge to smile, as the corners of my mouth lift in a barely discernible sign of one.

I say it with pride, and an overwhelming conviction, my shoulders set straight, ready to take on this insurmountable weight that I know I can. "I do. Claralis is mine to protect until my dying breath. On my honor and with my life, I swear to protect each and every one of my people." I feel settled in my mind. *My people.*

Wheln raises his head to the crowd, but lets the essence of his gaze remain on me, his voice elevating to a calm resonance. "Then, with my current authority, I relinquish my post of commander to you, and present to you with the title of Commander Liela Fiera Cordre, head of Claralis' armies, and in charge of its defense and protection. May you lead us well, and may you carry my blessing."

Wheln takes from the nearby podium, sitting in the center of the dais, a case with the seal of Claralis etched over the hinge—a snow-white dove carrying a crystal-blue flower, lines of the wind pushing weightlessly under its wings. He turns and offers it to me with a graceful reverence, nodding his approval as I lightly open the lid on the case, my fingers tingling as I withdraw an eloquently crafted rapier— the handle is crystal white and the blade a delicately sharp, mirror-glazed silver, glistening like the whites of a thousand snowflakes dancing in a wintry morning. While it has a simple eloquence, I am sure it's finely crafted, and just as practical as it is beautiful. I hold it vertical for a moment, admiring it in sheer disbelief.

And then I sheath it at my side, in my newly acquired scabbard of twining silver and white.

"I proclaim you, Liela Fiera Cordre, my formal successor from this moment on." His voice carries far, matched with the resounding cheers of the audience, and I finally lift my head to the raucous wave, goosebumps forming all over as my heart is set soaring, feeling the utter weightlessness of a realized dream.

Commander Wheln gives an incline of his head, and I turn to Driena, who also inclines hers and steps onto the dais. "Driena Laurel Tollus," I declare, "as my first act as Commander, I make the request that you be my second, to lead alongside me. You have all the qualifications that I myself have." I let myself smile this time, my eyes gleaming as she grounds me. "Will you follow me and be my second?"

She smiles back and dips her head, her mouth forming the words of a solemn oath. "I will. I promise to walk this path with you, Liela, and to bear this burden. You have my eternal loyalty and all that I can offer."

I present her with another sword, leaning lower against the dais, a rapier like mine, shining with the same eternal radiance, this one with lily green etched into the grip. "Then I proclaim you my second in Command of Claralis' armies, Driena Laurel Tollus."

Her fingers wrap around the grip with a thoughtful touch, and she lowers the blade to her side, dipping her head. She turns with determination to the watching audience, as a second wave goes through the crowd.

And she stands there, looking on with a mixture of gratitude, and a grim smile at the weight she has taken up. I know I will need her, and part of me wonders whether she should have been Commander instead. But, either way, I still would have stood nearly as close to her. She would have picked me to be by her side, just as surely as I picked her.

I leave the ceremony with my head held high. My heart blazes with an enveloping. I chose the life of a leader that protects her people, a Commander of my father's army.

My father allowed this, gave me the choice, and for that, I cannot express my unfathomable gratitude.

My sister has a choice too—to be the future leader, as I, the first heir to my father, have chosen a different path. However, she could also yield both the command of the city and the army to me, a burden that I would be willing to take for my sister, who does not desire that weight and power.

I spot Dunet as a burst of agile white, running out to greet me from the complex.

For a moment, I let go of formality and rush to embrace her, letting her spark spill into my mind as she clutches warmly at me with her tiny hands.

"I am so proud of you, Sister!" she whispers in my ear as we embrace.

I squeeze her tighter, caught up in the softness of this moment. I let go after the brief embrace, holding her at arm's length and giving her a warm smile that she returns, before I let go again.

Father stands behind Dunet, a twinkle in his eyes that few can recognize. He is proud, and my breast seems full enough to burst at the tenderness held in his gaze. Mother stands beside him, a hesitant smile crossing her features as she holds herself there in a loose grace. I think she is proud too, even if she finds no joy to say it. At least, that is what I would like to think.

I incline my head to Father. All the while, a slight grin sits on my face.

~

I find myself back at the barracks. Before I can set foot into the welcoming glow, through the pale dusk, Myllia is on top of me, her arms encircling me and her voice rising to a squeal. "I am so happy for you, Liela!"

My heart leaps in her arms. "You're suffocating me, Myllia," I say in a muffled voice, and she draws away hurriedly. "It felt good, though." I step in to hug her, softening my cheeks as my eyes grow tender.

Her cheeks redden to a deep shade, and she pulls away much more gently. She gives a clumsy curtsy. "I will see you soon ... Commander." I see a twinkle in her eyes as her words soften towards the end. "I really liked watching you today."

My heart locks up and I reach out as she twirls away, feeling a simultaneous rise, and fading, in my heart. I cannot help but laugh as her name leaves my lips, surprising even me. My heart thumps recklessly, and my mind searches for an answer to the sudden flame running through me, eluding all sense of my self-control.

I only have moments to think about it, before I am swarmed by what seems like the entirety of the barracks. My heart soars again, granted in a different way—these are my companions and, now, my men and women to lead.

Yet, I keep that haunting, tender warmth in the back of my mind. My skin still prickles with Myllia's touch.

~

Later, I find Darnor at the edge of the crowd. The sight of him fills me with peace, through all the clamor. As thrilling as it got, exhaustion now drags at my mind.

I fight the growing smile on my lips, as I make my way towards him. I grin as I get closer, saying, "You look pleased, Darnor."

His eyes settle on me kindly. "You deserve this. I think you can admit that."

"You know, I don't like to. Still ... I admit that it's hard not to feel good." I move beside him, looking on over the crowd.

"You don't think you might be putting that a little tamely?" He releases a breathy laugh.

"I am sorry, Darnor. I do feel very light right now. In some regards, I don't believe this is happening."

He chuckles, a meaningful light in his eyes. "That is because you always sold yourself short."

I shrug. "Maybe. Darnor, why do you not go enjoy yourself? I know I am glad to have you, but you *do* have a few suitors waiting ..." I tease amiably.

He somehow holds his voice, and I roll my eyes. "I appreciate it, Liela. But, you know, I would rather spend tonight with a friend. I find myself exhausted."

"I can say that for both of us." I grin, my shoulders sagging. I lean into the wall, closing my eyes for a moment, and shift them intently towards the celebration. "And I appreciate it."

"I really am glad you fulfilled your dream."

I shake my head. "It's not done yet. But yes, it is a relief. Though being Commander never had to be part of it … I could not help aspiring to it, even so." Because it always stood in the recesses of my mind, like a shining light that I could not help but grasp at with the swell of my lofty ambitions … and I never stopped.

He lets go of his breath, giving me a tempered glare. "Sometimes, I envy your commitment."

My voice softens. "Darnor, I couldn't have gotten half this far without people to lean on. You know that." I give a crinkling of my lips. "Unfortunately, I cannot have you under my immediate supervision at my side. You unfortunately don't qualify …"

Darnor scoffs lightly. "Don't worry. I know that well enough."

I pause, looking at him with a kind directness. "Nevertheless, know that I want you by my side as a friend anyway." I say it sincerely, to one of the most understanding friends I could ask for.

"You know, I will. If you need me, I will."

I smile. I trust that Darnor would even let go, if he had to. He recognizes what I need all too well.

"About me not joining in. It is still your party."

I wave my hand. "And I am enjoying it right here." I glance over again, motioning to the pool of people. "Why do we not both go?"

He shrugs. "If you insist. Personally, I have grown a little less fond of parties."

I feel a flicker of amusement in my eyes. "I don't think you ever liked them."

"True, but I can at least pretend. They have their charm. Anywhere you want to go?"

"How about we look for Driena? I want some friendly company."

He sighs shoulders slightly tense. "If you insist."

"I know you like her." I push with a cool undercurrent to my tone.

"Hardly. She always scolds me."

I try to hide my smirk. "Come on." We move through the crowd, and I close my eyes once more at the overwhelming bloom of peace in my mind.

The Taste of Anxiety

Dunet

Liela is gone too much, and it stabs at me every time I think about it. Ever since she took command of the city, she has had little time for me, though she always tries her best and it brings cheerful bursts back into my shadowed heart for just the smallest of moments, before it's gone again, and my mind is scattered into oblivion.

I drop to the ground, cascading a short distance in the waving grasses, before letting out a bristling sigh. Any sparks I had seem tucked far too deep for me to notice, and the shadows only grow more suffocating.

Liela is gone. Without her, I am left in this looming darkness. I have nothing to fill my mind with, but the weight that I don't deserve to have entrusted in me.

I gaze up at the sky, giggling as I transform a normal-looking cloud into a cute-looking dog in my head, before that image glances back into plain hollowness.

I try humming to myself, but even that sounds dour. Eriena's gentle face pops into my head, and I prance my way to the stables, my sunny eyes peeking past these heavy clouds.

I reach the stables in a skip, calling out to Eriena, who turns her head with a perking whinny that brings out the flashings of my teeth. My mind is soothed by the sight of her familiar face.

I creak open the gate to Eriena's stable, and she nuzzles me, like the comfort of a pillow. I burst out in a giggle, my hand combing through her mane.

Then I saddle Eriena, and I lead her from the stable, or rather, she trots next to me closely, over the short, trimmed grass before the castle. Turning to the right, once we pass the gate, the gray sky covers us in a blanket, bristling air sending goosebumps over my skin. It feels both harsh and comforting, running a shiver up my skin, but at the same time, I feel like I am held and enclosed in a box, the gray sky a dark wall above.

I hop up, my feet catching in the stirrups as my hands fumble at her mane. It takes me several attempts to get up onto the saddle and sit taut, gaze searching the pale skyline, castle at my back, town in a clamoring lull ahead of me, and the field of grass Liela and I play in cresting in waves in the cool wind. The Kalltarris Mountains are settled over the horizon, and a fading gold calls in a slumber from a gap in the clouds, cradling their peaks in silent wonder. I turn Eriena towards the grassy field. My eyes settle on the grass— the field I share with both Liela and Eriena. I hold it close to me, finding myself tugged towards its billowing softness, the golden stocks blowing and churning, muted under the sky.

I press against Eriena's flank, releasing a small laugh as I let her ride circles and swirls through the waving fields of muted gold.

My mind is shifting so rapidly recently, with all the looming responsibilities chasing at my back. I yearn so much to float away from them. I desperately want to handle them, and have grasped that I need to do so, to take that extra burden off my sister, but unlike her, that sense of responsibility is foreign to me. I reach for it, for Liela, only to let it slip from my trembling fingers again and again.

A tear grates down my face.

That cold emptiness presents itself, opening further as I swim above its depths, still at the surface, but I am slowing. My sister has left me ... yet I know she did not, and she never would. I need her to stay with me.

My nails clench at the reins, and I pull us back to the stable, giving Eriena a gentle pat as I lean over her mane. I fold my arms around her neck, whispering into her ear. "Thank you, Eriena. That was wonderful! I want you to know that you cheered me up."

She whinnies with a flick of her ears.

And then, to my delight, my eyes light on Liela. She waits for me in front of the stable, her eyes rimmed in shadow, but still bright once they meet mine. My breath catches at how exhausted she looks. I know her future rests on me.

Liela

For a moment, I thought I saw a shadow in my sister's eyes, and I was unable to find her pure shine ...

For just a moment, that spark was gone, and my heart stopped ...

But I veil my worry, locking that look out of my heart and bringing a tenderness to my own eyes, so that she can see it. I cast my concern aside, as soon as I see her carefree smile ... dismiss that initial shade for nothing, just a glancing illusion, for it must have been.

She bounds off Eriena and flurries over to me like a spry angel, untouched by darkness, her cheeks pink as a spring bloom. "Liela!" Her embrace softens my heart, yet her tone seems clutched ... as if there is a shrill note there that I have never picked up on before.

I run from my concern again, turning my back to it. "I thought you would be here," I say, brushing at her hair.

She beams wonderfully ... and I finally notice the tightness to her mouth.

I have barely seen her these past few days, yet I know she would tell me if she needed something ... I feel a twisting in the back of my throat ... No, whatever she is feeling, I cannot bring it up.

"I thought you were too busy today." Dunet's eyes glance up at me and they pull me back to the present.

"I was, but not for you." And with that, I see a lightening glow past that veil of her eyes. And it cuts at my heartstrings with agonizing sharpness.

Then, in an instant, all traces of that shadow dissipate to the wind, and I see her again as she always is. No, I can never let my fear of losing the Dunet I know settle in my heart, and I tuck it away, knowing she has not and could never change ... I know that spark would never waver ...

Why then do my eyes sting?

A Swelling of Love

Liela

I set down my quill, resting my hand against the desk. My new position has demanded a great deal of transitionary paperwork. I know that it's just the beginning, and I have been at this paperwork for hours today. There is so much Commander Wheln had to deal with, behind closed doors.

I lean back against my chair, playing my fingers along the desk and glancing sidelong out the window.

I want to see Myllia. My heart is drawn to her. I suppose I can give myself a break. For now, I can justify to myself that I deserve it. I felt ... a tug in my chest last time I saw her.

If only I could see her more, but if anything, I feel like she has been shoved to the side and it is like the breaths of clarity in my day are gone.

I stand and push my chair back, making up my mind that, of course, I want to see her. I will get back to everything later. If anything, I try to stay ahead of my workload, so I don't find this diversion a problem, as long as I keep up that mindset.

In truth, she told me I might find her in one of the courtyard-facing towers, if it were too cold for her to go outside.

I parse my lips. Somehow, I find it hard to see Myllia enjoying herself inside. It does not suite her.

Caroline Sophia Hamel

I push my chair under my desk.

Well, it was Wheln's old desk, which mixes strangely in my chest. But the wood is well-worn and sturdy, modest and strong, fitting for the station.

I have not the heart to alter the office myself. I still consider it Wheln's. I did bring the flower crown Dunet gave me, doing my best to preserve it in a little brown box, etched with a flower and scented with a preservative. Other than that, the office is still largely untouched and still in his image, which I don't mind—I don't need anything elaborate.

I stride out, my steps striking softly on the wood floor of the office and then muffling onto the carpets, as I overlook the spread of the enormous hallway running between the two halves of the library.

I make my way down the stairs and across the wide hall, several people nodding respectfully as they pass me. I make sure to give them a nod back. I know that I will have to get used to this. Everyone knows me now, and it's almost nerve wracking. Now I am also worried about intimidating people. I hope I don't, personally, because I want everyone to see themselves in me—to see that really, I am not much different.

Walking beneath a set of stone pillars, I cross out into the main hall. Everything seems a bit muted today, as the snow has started to fall on Claralis. Even so, I look onward with clarity.

I make my way up a staircase to the right, which leads up to a landing encircling the main room, and I turn off it after a brief expanse, sorting through the intricacies of the halls between the courtyards, then over the top of one of the walls separating the two. With a stiffening of my back, I brace myself against the cold. Flecks of snow drift across my vision, but not enough to pile up substantially.

I make my way into the opposing tower, heading up a short flight of stairs. Then I pause, one foot settled on the landing, and I feel a weight release from my mind.

A plush chair sits on the landing, under the winding of the staircase—royal purple over elegant wood, overlooking a tall window that is curved at the top, set into the stone. Myllia sits there on the other side of the small, curvaceous tower room.

I take a moment, and then walk up behind her, my footfalls softening. Myllia sits with her back to me, gazing out the window, the sky descending into a lovely violet. Her hands lay folded over her lap, a faraway look on her face. I almost don't want to disturb her, but I am pulled in by the waves of our memories lapping at my mind, and so I go towards her. She looks so peaceful and pleasant, sitting how she is.

I come up beside her, laying a hand on her shoulder. I feel a slight tremor in her body as she startles at my presence, though she swiftly turns to me and relaxes, giving me a radiant smile. "Liela," she begins, her voice calm.

"You have that faraway look in your eyes again," I say. "You were always the daydreamer, Myllia. I thought I might find you up here."

"I was waiting for you." She meets my eyes more clearly, gently. "I like sitting in the courtyard, and sometimes

I don't mind the cold, but I thought I would come up here. Liela, you know that this is such a different feeling, looking on the courtyard and the sunset from this angle ..." Her eyes stay on me, though, sweet as honey.

There's something about it ... but more than that, Myllia glows exquisitely. Her wisteria and rose dress flatter her perfectly, flowing over the edges of the chair in passionate ripples, cutting low at her chest, and backless, in a way that makes my breath catch. "It is a beautiful view," I struggle to say, struck silly by her beauty. "You have not been waiting here too long, have you?"

She giggles, pressing her hand to her lips, before letting it fall. "Of course not." She turns back to the window for a moment. "Just passing the time. You have so many important things to attend to, I was not sure when you would come. You are Commander now, after all." With a touch of anxiety, she looks me up and down, over the decorum of my station. I find myself glad that it's in my favorite color, and I am also glad that Myllia believes it suits me.

I avert my eyes at her look but try not to call too much attention to it. "I am not busy enough that I could not see you. That is why I came here, of course. I have no obligations this evening."

Myllia's cheeks turn rosy, and she meets my eyes. "Liela, I was ..." She clasps her hands tighter, her chest rising. "I was wondering if we could dine together tonight."

My heart stutters and I smooth it over quickly, her question catching met off guard. I have eaten with Driena and Darnor plenty, so this should be ... normal. Yet my mouth feels dry. My blood rushes with a strange feeling, a tingling that runs up my spine. And the words automatically leave mouth. "Why, of course! You're my friend, after all." I hold out my hand in a formal manner.

Myllia reaches up to grab it delicately, her smooth fingers overlapping mine. Her hand is warm and comforting and she gives me another brilliant smile. "I would love that."

Myllia insists that she prepare herself before dinner and I feel the tickle fading from my hand as she takes hers off mine, looking at me from under her stunning lashes. "You should change too."

I give her an unsure smile, as she swivels away, casting her eyes back at me one more time. Her graceful step seems more ... tentative than normal.

I make my way into my room, but when I get to my closet, I pause, not knowing what to look for. My fingers hover over the few clothes I have, and I grab clumsily at a navy-blue formal suit, open at the front with a white, matching formal shirt underneath to pair. Still, I hesitate. Is this really enough? I shake my head again, before undressing and pulling on my attire. I also slip on slim white boots, with minimal heels, and equally white gloves. I pull my hair back, looping it into a neat ponytail.

Then I stop in front of my mirror, biting my lip as I look at my plainness—I look too straight and dignified for the moment. I wonder if I should be wearing something different ...

But what else could I wear?

I feel so ... awkward.

My heart begins to pound, and I shake my head, trying to reason with myself that there's nothing to worry about.

I breathe ... This is fine.

And I know that there should be no reason to be nervous.

It's *Myllia*.

I press my palm to my chest, feeling light for a moment. I bite my lip. Then, turning away from the mirror, I hide from my image. What more could I do?

I meet Myllia at the bottom of the stairs to the front of the castle and my breath catches with amazement. I feel a deep yearning to move forward, even if I feel locked in place by the mere sight of her.

She stands there in a frilly dress of an amazingly deep and dark, passionate red, backless and highlighting her plentiful breasts and all her curves. Her hair is combed to perfection. Her lips are done sumptuously in matching red makeup, and her eyes are highlighted just enough to draw even more attention to them. The gloves she wears pull up between her elbow and her shoulder, in dazzling scarlet, combined with lavender heels, open and laced across with straps. She looks absolutely stunning ...

She looks ... perfect.

Absolutely perfect.

I take a trance-like step forward, as if I am floating on a cloud and she is a dream.

Myllia gives me a twirl. "How do I look?"

I pause for a second, not knowing what to say. "Absolutely stunning ... You look beautiful, Myllia." At that she beams, and I cannot help returning a grin of my own. I almost laugh at the giddy feeling in my chest.

"Come on." She gives a short hop in her heels—I think it's cute—before gently grabbing my arm, but I sense a sizzling excitement in how she holds me. And I let myself be pulled along, feeling the magical rush of the air, as snow dances around us. I realize I am smiling just as much at her happiness as I am mine.

I want to soar with her.

When she waves her arm at an extravagant carriage, I stop short, my eyes going wide.

She turns back to me, wringing her gloved fingers together. "Well, you see, I put something together for us." She brings her hand up to her curls, pulling them away from her ear and smiling at me with an overwhelming fondness. "If you want to go." Then, she offers me her hand.

"Myllia ... this is perfect ..." And it is so perfect that I find it hard to comprehend. What lengths has she gone to, to put this together for us? "Myllia ..." I reach for her hand, and two attendants rush to open the door. She turns, lifting her head and giggling as we walk together, and I have the strange urge to do the same, my cheeks feeling hotter with each passing moment.

I mount the steps, and the door closes behind us. I catch a brief glimpse at Myllia, and then I turn away as the carriage starts, the lights and the snow blinking past us.

It is only a moment until we are in town and at our destination.

I step out and offer my hand to Myllia. She follows me daintily, holding up the corners of her dress.

Once we are both grounded, I glance up at a sign through the lanterns, the snow dusting at my feet. It looks quaint. The Little Candle.

Myllia reaches for my hand again and draws a bit closer to me, the softness of her breath feeling oddly close to my cheek.

We pass through the door into the dimly lit restaurant, and an orange glow is cast on wavering shadows from numerous candles and a flaming hearth in the wall. A musician plays a harp in one corner, complementing the soothing atmosphere. "This is a nice place you picked out, indeed."

"Very pretty," Myllia remarks, scanning the room with a light in her eyes. "A friend of mine picked it out for me."

"Your friend has very ... shall I say, romantic tastes." My blood feels on a borderline of hot and cold, but I also feel pulled in by the quiet notes in my ears.

"I would say so." Myllia smiles with a giggle, twirling halfway on her heel to look at me. "I reserved a table over there." She presses her hand further into mine and looks into my eyes, imploring me to follow, and I move, as if I am in a dream.

Myllia plops onto the seat, shifting to get comfortable, and then rests the back of her hand against her cheek, cocking her head and giggling. Her eyes look at me warmly. "Well, what do you think?"

I hardly have any words. We sit tucked into the corner, the harp player in view, fingers gracing the strings with precision. I shake my head. "It really is too much, Myllia …"

She seems to take me in with her eyes. "You know how pretty you are, Liela?"

I look down. I really don't.

Myllia leans forward, smiling sweetly. "Liela, you are the most beautiful, kind, honest person I know."

"All of that could apply to you as well, Myllia."

"Maybe, but to me, it describes you." She turns to a waitress approaching our table. "Hello, Pricillia."

"Myllia," the waitress croons with a delighted air. "What can I get for the two of you?"

"Hmm …" She looks at me. "Just water tonight … for a little luck. I wouldn't want anything to be ruined."

Pricillia looks at me too, asking, "And for you?"

"The same." I usually avoid drink, except for special occasions, like special friend time with Driena and Darnor, or celebrations. Still … I thought maybe Myllia would …

The waitress leaves and I reach for my water. "You didn't want anything?"

She takes a sip. "Not tonight, really. Some moments are special, and I find I remember them better this way. I also find myself happier, though I am not opposed to glasses every few nights. I am used to having them around formal occasions and with my family. I am a lady, after all."

I grin, picking up my own glass. "You have been here before?" I feel a slight drop in my stomach as I say it.

Her glass pauses halfway to the table. "Only on my own. I wanted to come here with someone, eventually." She looks at me meaningfully, fluttering her eyelashes. "And I was hoping that that person would be you."

I feel flustered.

The waitress, Pricillia, comes back. She is a girl in her mid-twenties, and she has tied her dark hair in a ponytail, revealing her freckled face. She gives us a dashing smile, which complements her nicely trimmed, black-and-white suit with coattails, and matching black slacks and high heels. "Anything you're ready to order?"

Myllia eyes her menu, finger poised over the page. "I think I will have the scallops with your specialty sauce." The scallops would have been harvested and transferred here from the Sea of Valaheir, to the south.

"And for you?"

"The portobello risotto with chevre and roasted vegetables please."

She jots down a few notes and flashes a charming smile. "Your order will be ready soon."

"Thank you, Pricillia."

I turn back to Myllia, but feel an uncertainty of where to look and what to say.

"You know, I find it funny when you flush."

Oh ... I pull my legs closer to me beneath the table.

"Never mind that, then." Her eyes look questioning, and she squirms again. "Sorry, Liela. You know I do get stage fright sometimes. I am guessing you do as well. In fact, I think it is written all over you."

My eyes jump to her ... I always thought I hid it. But, maybe not around her. "Myllia, I think you can be bolder than you give yourself credit for."

"Oh, I can." She gives a full, irresistible smile. "When I want to be. I find you help me with that. You know that you are an inspirational person."

I shrug it off, but feel a rush at the compliment. "I hope I can be."

"You are. And, Liela ..." She hesitates, pulling at the sleeve of her glove. "Have you ... been with anyone?"

My breath catches. "What do you mean?"

"Oh, nothing," she giggles out. "That was all. I don't think I needed to ask that one, really. I just wanted to tease you."

"Oh ..." My ears feel hot.

She swirls her drink, and I find myself staring, entranced, to which she flits her eyelashes yet again. I find myself blinking, but this time, I am not able to look away. "Liela," she mouths, then covers her mouth with her gloved hand, giggling again.

Not much later, the food comes, and everything goes by pleasantly, until it's done. Then, I feel awkward again, my skin tingling uncomfortably.

Myllia glances at me, before she rises elegantly. It takes me a moment to notice her hand extended towards me, a visible blush to her cheeks.

A violin player and pianist join the harp player, all three now playing a soft, slow melody, gradually rising in gentle swells.

Myllia hesitates for a moment, and I look curiously at her outstretched hand, before it dawns on me, just a second before she puts it into words. "Will you ... dance with me, Liela?" It is still timid, but firm in its resolve ... Sure. Her other hand lingers passively on the frills of her dress, and I can tell that she is nervous. My own heart picks up, and I feel a clogging in my throat.

She looks lovely, and my heart stirs at her offer. "Yes," I say softly, the only answer I can possibly give to her. I think I can tell that I want to be with her right now, even if the racing in my heart feels like an elusive longing. That longing is for the lady right here in front of me. Myllia.

I take her hand and return that lovely smile with my own. "I can dance the male part," I say, with traces of hesitancy.

Her face blooms, and I nearly hyperventilate as I look upon her, as stunning as she is. We lead each other onto the floor and begin. I feel every pulse in my heart, every note of the music, and I feel the strong urge to pull closer to her.

It lasts minutes ... or hours. I can't tell, but I feel at peace. I know how right and perfect the world is in this moment.

However, we both realize it is the last dance of the night.

Myllia tucks her head into my shoulder, her curls tickling against my neck. "Is this all right, Liela?"

I feel a clump in my throat. "Yes. It is, Myllia." I release a tautness from my chest, relaxing into her and letting go of any fears I have. Because, right now, I feel so certain, my heart cradled by Myllia's touch. And I find that I don't ever want to let go.

I feel so utterly weightless, immersed in the lights and the music, that I close my eyes too.

And I feel the beat of her heart against mine, so sure and grounding ... I don't know how I never realized just how lovely she is ... and how I could never see how truly settled my world could feel with her this close.

To Hold a Flower

A Cradle of Love

Liela

I take a deep breath, my eyes lingering on the window.

My hand shakes slightly, and I just breathe for a moment.

My eyes close and I can see Myllia's luscious, gentle, kind form there, her hand extended to me and a smile playing on her lips.

I know what I want.

I hardly understand it myself, but I know that there's something calling out in my heart for release, as surely as I have understood anything.

I shove my chair back abruptly, frowning down at it, then I laugh, a shakiness at the edge of my vocal cords.

I take another deep breath to calm myself.

What to do? What to say?

I close my eyes as I pass towards the courtyard, clearly remembering the press of her touch, the feel of her hair, and the jostling of my heart.

My hand squeezes, as if wanting to hold her hand again, so gentle, yet so sure.

I know Myllia understands what she wants far better than I do ...

I just need to talk to her and sort out everything for myself.

I find Myllia in the courtyard, as she usually is. I startle at the clarity in her gaze, as she casts a playful, serene look over her shoulder. That wistful look is gone; her body exudes confidence as she eyes me. She seems so ... present.

And her expression reminds me of the way she looked at me last night.

She is wearing the same yellow dress as when we first met. That pads against my heartstrings.

She looks so plain and simple and pretty, far less adorned than last night, but somehow far more beautiful ...

Then, she runs to me, as if embraced by the love of the wind, throwing her arms around me. She steps back, her eyes wandering, as she starts reaching for her dress. She looks so shy, so expectant. She blinks at me meaningfully, pulling just far enough away that I feel a yearning at the distance.

She pulls at her fingers. "The other night ... It meant a lot." She stumbles over her words, but her insistence on each one is clear.

I respond unthinkingly. "It was special to me too." And My own bluntness surprises me, and I feel the sparks of building anticipation.

She looks directly at me, steadying her breath, pulling her hands from the creases of her dress. "Liela ..." She gives me a true, unguarded smile, more lovely than any summer's day and more precious than any star. "I love you."

Time freezes for a moment ... even my heartbeat. I feel an unfamiliar sensation, and a shiver up my spine—a feeling that makes me ascend. I feel so light ... so ... hot ...

Myllia seems to find the answer in my eyes. She hesitates for a moment, mouthing my name, then she pulls in, her mouth meeting mine.

I relax, feeling like nothing else matters, savoring the touch of her lips. They feel so right, blanketing my heart in an ethereal bliss.

Love. My heart swells in confirmation. That was what I was feeling and what I had always felt for her, hidden in the longings of my mind, but until now, it was too afraid to surface.

Gently, I pull away, filled with passion and heat. I love her. I smile more genuinely than I ever have; it feels like my cheeks will burst. "I love you too, Myllia ... I love you so much."

Her eyes meet mine with a fierce softness, their cornflower tone so incredibly lovely, as I finally realize how truly gentle their depths are. I see my reflection in their compassionate light.

She rises on her tiptoes and jumps straight into my arms, her lips again connecting with mine, only this time with an electric passion. Her arms encircle me, and I wrap mine around her. She slows down, and we savor a softer, longer intimacy; it is nearly eternal. Filled with love, living a dream that I never even knew I wanted. I close my eyes and let her breath and body take me wherever she wants to go.

I am not sure how long it lasts, or how long we stand there before pulling away, swirling together in a daydream. My heart still feels full enough to burst, and my blood pumps inside me with incredible delicateness, urging me to stay here forever.

Now I understand everything I have been feeling for her, and everything I wanted ...

And I just feel ... so alive, utterly burning with energy.

I look upon her heated cheeks and the warmth in her eyes. They are impossibly deep, shining in a radiance that I love dearly—she is dearer to me than any other.

Myllia giggles.

Neither of us need any words, as we stare into each other's eyes.

Her cheeks are still red. She looks so pretty, so beautiful. My breathing is composed once more, yet I am still bathed in this moment, everything else fading from my vision except for her.

"Liela ..." she whispers my name tenderly.

I sit with Myllia beside the pond, her head against mine.

I wonder if I will wake up to find that everything has faded, but it never does, no matter how many times I blink.

Myllia turns her eyes up to me, a prying look, as she remains plastered to my shoulder. I rest into her.

"I can see why you like it here. It is so peaceful. Now it reminds me of you." I hold my breath, almost laughing at my boldness ... still so new to me.

She crinkles her nose, giving a, "Tee-hee!" Then, her face relaxes again. "It reminds me of you too. Why do you think I come here every day?"

I can see the teasing light in her eyes, and I raise mine at that, before breaking into my own uncontrollable laugh that flutters into a giggle, feeling so free in the sound and feel of it, in a way I never thought I could.

"You may be Commander, but your laugh is just as lovely as always."

I resist the urge to blush, but I can feel the tingling of my cheeks anyways.

A pleasant silence passes between us, the only sound the brush of air on the crystalized grasses, shimmering in the morning dawn.

Myllia pulls her head up, a slight shake in her voice. "What do we do now?"

I frown. "What do you mean?"

"I just ... I think it was sudden for you. If I am being honest, I was certain about this for some time. What I mean is, are you ready to tell people?"

I pause, for only a moment, before a smile plays at my face. "Well, I would like you to meet Dunet. She deserves to know more than anyone." I feel at peace in my mind. "You will love her, and I know she will love you, as I am sure Father will." I give a long sigh. "And Mother will like you too, I just don't know how she will react. It might be … hard."

Myllia squeezes my hand to comfort me, setting my heart at ease once more.

I pause, asking uncertainly, "What about you?"

She smiles faintly. "I do not have anyone close enough that I feel like telling." She shakes her head slightly, as if trying to reassure me. "I really do not care. It does not matter, as long as I am with you." She gives a bittersweet smile and my heart melts. "I will love you always, Liela."

Happiness bursts inside me, even if there is a fading feeling rising along with it. Nothing else matters. I am with the one I love. I feel a crushing in my heart a moment later, though, my sister coming to my mind. Isn't she that person to me … more than Myllia?

But it is quickly lost, as I am enveloped by Myllia's warmth. Serenely, I listen to the sound of her heartbeat.

To Be Torn Apart

Liela

In the haze of midmorning, I stare sidelong at Myllia, my hand curling around hers.

My lips bloom into a smile, just waiting for the mushy feeling in my chest, which will surely come when I finally introduce her to Dunet. Even if I hesitate a moment, I give a small knock on Dunet's door.

I hear the patter of her footsteps a second later, and she swivels the door open, cocking her head, and peering at us. Her gaze settles on our entwined fingers, before she looks back up to me.

I offer her a smile that tugs generously at its edges, even if a chill runs over me. "Dunet, this is Myllia." It comes out much calmer than the swirling of my heart.

Dunet offers a brilliant smile, like a flower full of sunshine. "She's your friend?"

I squirm, just barely. "She is ... Yes, she is my friend, a very special friend," I reply with warmth, looking sidelong at Myllia. "Though she isn't as good a *friend* as you," I add, turning a slightly different smile towards Dunet, yet no less loving.

Out of the corner of my eye, I can see a lush red blush on Myllia's cheeks.

Dunet looks at Myllia for another moment, then complete acceptance spirals in a broad smile, even if I don't think she can understand the depth of our feelings. She beams, casting her eyes up, and then away with a short hop. "Will you be my friend too?"

Myllia lowers herself, so she is on her knees to be level with Dunet. "Of course, I will." My heart stirs at the adorable sight of them. I couldn't imagine anyone kinder in the world that I would rather be with.

Dunet's smile swells with a wondrous light as her eyes shine. Then, she rushes in for a hug. Myllia's eyes flutter wide in surprise, before she closes them and hugs Dunet back.

Myllia pulls away lightly. "Liela told me all about you, you know?"

"Really?" Dunet's voice lifts.

"To be honest, I was a little jealous." She eyes me, that part sounding teasing somehow. "But I am so glad to meet you, Dunet."

Dunet flushes as she looks away, but rocks back-and-forth on the pads of her feet.

She looks so happy, and it stirs at me warmly. But that moment from the other day ... that look I thought I saw in Dunet's eyes ... still threads its way into my conscience.

I thought I would not dwell on it, but why do my eyes find it hard to settle on her? Why am I thinking about it now? I thought I knew her every emotion. Dunet looks back at me with a still swirling light, and I attempt to hide that thought from my mind. "Why don't the three of us go on an adventure?"

Dunet looks curiously at Myllia.

Myllia lightly grasps the hem of her skirt, something I have noticed she tends to do when she is in thought, nervous, or embarrassed, and that warm ember sparks within my chest, to be able to read her. In this moment, she is thinking, and I know she takes Dunet's expectations seriously.

Her face brightens momentarily as she turns a smile back to Dunet. "How about we go to the shopping district?" She poses, fingers settled over her cheek. "I would like to try some dresses on for Liela while I am there." She gives a suggestive, heated blush that turns my stomach, sending a ripple down my spine as I shift in my posture.

Dunet glosses over the change in Myllia's tone. She looks back at me, her eyes bright. "Can we, Liela?"

Fortunately, I have a few days off, before my duties as Commander take hold of my schedule. I kneel and brush my fingers over her hair. "Of course, we can, Dunet."

I take her hand and let her pull me down the hall, then down the stairs into the bustling main entrance, before we finally step outside.

Myllia draws ahead of us at the gate, flagging down a gold-trimmed carriage, with a glow that sends my heart aflutter. Every time she turns her gaze on me, it sends a playful chill across my body and a thrill into my heart.

Taking one window seat under the lush red curtains, Myllia then offers her hand to Dunet. She has me take the other side. Dunet bounces on the scarlet-cushioned seat as we pull out, polished wood squeaking underneath her tiny frame. She glances out the window with wide eyes as the world whisks by.

Soon, the carriage rolls to a stop and Myllia gracefully leads herself out, in a flowing mustard dress, with buttons along the chest and a white ribbon around her middle. My breath catches as she casts her twinkling eyes back at me.

Dunet hops out, hands behind her back.

I take the steps with still faltering breaths, taking Myllia's hand. Goosebumps run up my arm. Myllia draws towards me for a moment, before glancing at Dunet and turning away, letting go of me as she grasps for one of Dunet's small hands. I follow her, and reach down to pull on Dunet's other hand, looking down at my sister with a touching smile. We lead her along the crowded streets, which are uncommon in most cities this far north. In Mathar, at least.

The wind is blustery today, but not yet freezing, the clouds gray. In the shadow of the Kalltarris Mountains, most of the year is rain and cold snow, and it gets dark quite early in the winter. I wonder how Myllia isn't freezing. Dunet wears a gray fleece coat over her white dress, and for once, cute honey-brown boots to match her honey hair.

Tents and stalls are set up below the gray skyline, interspersed between bright, quaint shop windows. The residential areas fade into the back alleys, away from the main thoroughfare, which is padded down in dirt from numerous people's shoes. Most of the city's bustle flows along this wide thoroughfare, an occasional boxed carriage drawn by two steeds pulling a member of the nobility or upper-class families down the center of its width. The castle and the Kalltarris Mountains along the skyline draw up loftily at our backs, while it opens distantly on one end into wide fields that gently rise to meet the rolling hills and barren forests cradled in frost.

We pass between the stalls, Dunet's eyes widening at the goods on display. Her small hand is tightly bound to mine. Myllia's eyes skim along the stalls, until she spots a dress shop. Then, glancing sidelong at me, her gaze makes my heart beat rapidly. It wasn't so long ago when Myllia was just a friend, someone who I could never have realized my true feelings for, until she put them into such cradled words. Of course, we are still friends, yet I have a new thrill in my heart, something more and new that seems so normal ... if it was anyone else. But she just melts my heart into utter weightlessness.

"I know a store around here that a friend of mine works at. Dunet, you don't mind if I leave you there for a short time while Liela and I stop at the dress store?" Myllia asks her. Dunet's eyes seem to fade just a little ... again, I cannot read that expression. It is as if she is hiding something, or maybe I just cannot see it. My breath locks at the trembling of my hands.

Myllia's sweet voice flutters at my thoughts again, tugging me away, even as the current of Dunet's eyes still tosses at me. "I will take you there, and I will be back with Liela before you know it." Dunet's eyes come to a rest, even with a slight shine, but I can see a cloud stinging behind their depths. Is there hurt too?

Yet, it's as if she pushes these darker feelings aside. "I don't mind!" It sounds slightly shrill, even as she layers her words brightly. Before I can say anything, she turns around and rushes off. Myllia reaches over and squeezes my hand softly, before she follows Dunet.

I gaze at them, my eyes moistening slightly at their edges, before they are lost in the crowd. But I cannot bring myself to follow, my legs feeling rooted, like I would collapse if I tried. Besides, I trust Myllia, or maybe that is just an excuse to blind myself from whatever is going on in Dunet's mind.

Myllia returns shortly after, giving me a tender smile that touches dearly against my strangled heart. "She is fine," she murmurs lightly, reaching to my hand and giving it a light squeeze.

My voice catches. "Are you sure?"

Myllia's eyes cloud as she traces her finger along the creases of her dress, meeting mine as unwaveringly as she can. "I wish I could say yes, but it is something I think you need to talk to her about yourself."

I stay silent as my breathing picks up, heartbeat racing out of control.

In that silence, Myllia gently pulls me towards the dress shop. It may be something selfish that twists horribly in my stomach, but I let Myllia lead me away from Dunet, let that moment slip by, replaced by the comfort of her touch.

~

We pass through the shining glass door into the quiet, shadowed radiance of the dress shop. Myllia twirls to face me with a giggle, her eyes playing a mirror against me. She holds both sides of her dress as she pivots on her heels, looking longingly at me from below her lashes. "This is just for you and me, Liela."

She turns back to the racks, gracing her hands along the fabric. "You can pick something if you want, Liela. I know that I really want you to ..."

She moves away and I take a halting step forward. My eyes settle on so many shades, and I reach my hand out. It pauses over the fabric. My mind searches, not knowing what I desire.

I slip into a slow walk, casting my fingers lightly on the fabric. Beams of cozy white are cast through the skylights, onto the corridor-like racks. Candles dance, encased in glass, and antique crystal chandeliers grace the ceiling.

My heart stirs in a quiet, rhythmic beat that drones against my mind. I turn in a daze, looking over the room.

"Liela." Myllia calls to me softly, and my heart jumps at the touch of her hand. Her smile wavers a bit at my reaction. "I did not mean to scare you. I was just going to try on a few dresses, and I wanted you to see them."

A small smile crosses my face, and I follow her towards the dressing room.

She stops, taking a breath. "I would have you come in, but ... I think I want to surprise you." Her fingers clench as her cheeks redden, the sight of which makes my heart stutter wildly. "And, well, maybe that is not the only reason ..."

My voice comes out dry. "Of course, Myllia."

She lets go of my hand and steps behind the door.

I wait outside the changing room, my eyes turning back to the racks as I try to myself from the unbearable hot feelings inside me. I was never into dresses, at least not in the same way that most girls were. I would wear them on occasion, and ... I suppose that in some ways, I liked them. I guess I always just took after Father.

That is just how I play it in my head.

Myllia opens the door moments later. She looks gorgeous, and for a moment, I'm speechless. Her dress is a light coral, featuring a crisscrossing, satin V-neck. It hugs her breasts as she breathes in and out deeply. The dress thinly rises over her shoulders, translucent frills descending just over them, opening backless. A wide belt wraps around her fat waist, beaded in silver. Then the hem descends over her chubby legs, just above her amber heels.

She presses her fingers against the swell of her lips, a brilliant blush over her cheeks. "Did I overdo it?"

"No, not at all. You're breathtaking, Myllia."

"I want you to try one on," Myllia murmurs to me with a flitting of her eyes.

My heart freezes for a moment.

"I want to pick it out," she adds, eyes fluttering.

I nod, giving my consent, even if my heart is pounding in my ears.

Myllia comes back minutes later with a dress of a beautiful, deep green. I take it, stepping into the room in a trance, eyes meeting my reflection in the mirror. I stare at the reedy, too-thin frame and firm features. Then, I remove my clothes and reach for the dress, feeling its soft, velvety fabric, before slipping it on. I stare at my own reflection with a perplexed rolling in my stomach, goosebumps forming on my arms.

"Even I have to admit," I whisper to myself, "her choice was perfect."

It fits over my slim frame with ease, even if I don't have the curves and fullness Myllia does. I suppose I like how it looks. Another shiver runs up my arms. Even if I am not entirely comfortable wearing a dress, especially one this revealing, I think that I can wear it for Myllia. Taking a breath, my eyes catch the slit by my leg, which is smooth and slender. I am taller than a lot of girls. And the toned curve of my calves is one thing that I do genuinely like about my appearance.

I step out, still in a daze. I feel so exposed, in a way I rarely do, yet I hold my shoulders in a composed manner, meeting Myllia's eyes. I can do this for the person I love. I keep my legs from trembling, my heart surging at the light of her gaze.

Myllia's breath seems to catch as she blushes at me, just as I blush at her. "You look stunning." The way she says it sends a thrill through my rigid chest. I smile, finding a renewed confidence in her words. I can be beautiful for her.

"I want to try something else on for you ..." she whispers, and it sends an excited shiver over my body.

My breath catches. I am pretty sure she is blushing more than I have ever seen her do so. She chose what I would assume is one of the most revealing dresses in the shop in her size—a dress of icy blue, thinly hugging her body, and ruffled in white veils. I suppress a laugh. She flushes such a rosy red that I just cannot stand it, and I bend forward in a laugh, my skin burning hot, and she finally giggles, in tears.

She was serious when she said it was just for me.

We exit the shop, hands entwined. Myllia convinced me to buy the dress ... and wear it. I cannot believe I caved into her insistence, but I just cannot resist her tender, prying smile as she flits her eyelashes at me, so alluring. I am not used to so much attention focused on my looks.

Myllia is in her dress as well. The coral one, of course. Her sunny smile flutters back to me every few moments. She grabs my hand, as if sensing my discomfort, even if her doing so draws a few looks that I must ignore.

We come to the sweet shop, in a lovely building on a corner of the thoroughfare and an alley. Several counters sit with wrapped candies and containers of fresh-made sweets, low enough for little, friendly touches from tiny hands.

Dunet is near the counter, being shown around by someone who I assume is Myllia's friend. The woman has black pixie hair, dark hazel eyes, creamy skin, a sharp nose, and soft lips. Her frame is thin, wiry, garbed by a sleek black suit over a white shirt and ruby red pants halfway from her knees to her ankles. I spot a set of ankle bracelets, and her light pink, lofted sandals.

Myllia's friend sneaks a piece of candy to Dunet. Then she swipes her head around a moment later with a full-lipped grin, looking at Myllia and me.

Acting like nothing just happened, she taps Dunet on the shoulder and points in our direction.

Dunet looks up with a gleam in her eyes. She runs over, cocking her head as she reaches us. "You're in a dress?"

"Yes ..." I suppress a blush. "Myllia picked it out for me."

"I love it!" she says, smiling widely.

I brush the compliment aside with a laugh, but it still settles in my heart. "Is there anything you want here?"

"No," she replies, turning her eyes down to her closed palm. I find a crinkling smile coming to my lips. After all, she was given the candy. "Helin showed me around!"

"She was very enthusiastic," Helin replies, sweetness lacing her words.

"It's nice to meet you. I take it you're Myllia's friend?"

Helin leans back against the counter, on her elbows with a flashing allure. "Yes. Acquaintance, more like it; Myllia comes here occasionally. Have you two known each other for a while?"

"Quite a while, yes. Myllia is a dear and longtime friend of mine."

"Glad to hear it. It's always good to see her."

"We are very close," Myllia adds, a little too seriously. Her eyes twinkle. I laugh internally at her attempt to seem casual about her feelings.

Dunet tugs at my hand.

"I think Dunet is ready to see more of the market. Thank you for treating her so well. Next time we will stop by longer."

We walk along the streets, Dunet ahead of the two of us. She looks back at me, a question in her eyes, and I feel uncertain. We have only gone a few paces outside the shop, and I am about to give a verbal reply to Dunet when we are approached by someone.

Recognition dawns in my eyes. It's Nivel, a fellow knight. His black hair is slicked back neatly, contrasting with his fair complexion, brilliant blue eyes, and a gentle nose over a slim mouth. No, I am his Commander now. I still have not gotten used to my new position.

Nivel stops before me, a little wide-eyed at seeing me in a dress. I think he almost laughs, but he holds it down, his eyes hardening. "Commander Cordre, an urgent matter has arisen and requires your input." My mindset shifts instantly, turning serious as I register his firm, official tone, and taut body language.

I glance at Dunet and Myllia, wanting to apologize. "I need to attend to this matter. Can you look after Dunet for me while I am gone, Myllia?"

In understanding, Myllia nods, and she holds onto Dunet's hand. "Of course, I will."

I hesitate with Dunet, feeling cold, almost cruel. "I am sorry, Dunet, but I have to leave you." She nods, and I hope she understands ... Of course, she does. I always do this these days. "I will see you as soon as I can. I love you." I reach forward to kiss her forehead and bring her into a hug. Her arms grasp weakly around my back. With that, I turn and leave the two of them behind.

I wait until we are out of the crowd and nearing the castle. Then, I ask, "What is it, Nivel?"

"A nearby village was attacked. Our proof is incomplete, but we believe it was an attack from the north."

I bite my lip. "You think it was from Arathulen?"

"It is likely." He grates his teeth, releasing a low sigh. "We've found signs of patrols and armed groups in the surrounding area."

I purse my lips. "They wouldn't dare, but perhaps ..." I slip into a contemplative silence, filtering through possibilities in my head, trying to avoid the worst one ... an invasion of Mathar.

"I never thought I would see you in a dress," Nivel pries, as if trying to lift the mood, but the comment only prickles unpleasantly at my skin.

"And?" I ask dryly.

"And it looks good on you."

I glare at him, letting go of an exasperated breath.

"Will I be seeing you in one more often?"

"That isn't how you address your new Commander, Nivel," I state firmly, my mental state already shifting back to the matter at hand.

He opens his mouth to counter smartly.

I give him a cold stare and he falters, seeming to realize his mistake and the change in my authority, which he should have respected in the first place. "Let us focus on the task at hand," I spell out clearly. "Remember that, Nivel." My face hardens. Just because I am with Myllia now, I cannot let my emotions carry me away. "This isn't a situation to make light of. It is neither the time, nor the place."

"Of course, Commander." He dips his head. "My apologies."

With that, his expression once again turns serious, and I nod. I am satisfied at his correction, though I may have to address the matter later, if it persists.

I gain a new steadiness, knowing that I can push through my own embarrassment to stand tall.

But once again, there is a lingering image of Dunet's reaching eyes, as she looks back on me walking away ...

The Tides of Dread

Liela

I stride into the lofted meeting room, set in a pentagon of gray-black stone and soaring marble columns at each crease of the wall, rising far to the ceiling. It is a cavernous, hollow room, but with an elegant, noble fireplace against one wall.

The elite knights and lords all straighten at my presence.

"Commander Cordre," comes Driena's soft, firm voice, like a settled bell in frost.

"Driena," I reply with a nod. "I want a detailed account on the incident."

"Yes, Liela." She lets go of my title, as I suppose I have too for her. It rings nicer than it should. Maybe I am a bit soft, but I find that it strengthens my focus, and I can center my breathing again. Unlike Nivel, she at least consistently addresses the tone of a situation. She motions to a seat at the table and draws her eyes to a large map, fingers set gracefully over the glass tabletop.

"They attacked here, in Nalton Village." Her pointer finger skims the map and taps over its surface. "Their presence has been detected slightly to the east and west as well, but so far, they have not moved farther south."

I nod, my mind, sorting through our options.

"Unfortunately, they were dressed simply, but their weapons were of a northern make, a craft close enough, we believe they are Arathulen soldiers. Of course, we have no conclusive proof."

I land on a not-so-distant memory of my mother addressing my family and I, for once, wishing I had followed up. I wonder if she would have told me if I were Commander already. I trust that she would have. "The supply lines have been inconsistent of late, too," my mouth parses. I wish that I had held onto that.

"Yes, it's quite possible that they're linked." Her eyes shimmer darkly. "And there's no reason to doubt that they are."

"Has anywhere else been attacked?"

"As far as we know, no. Though information travels slowly enough here that it could have happened." Lord Lux, a sultry-looking man with a curled mustache, intense amber eyes, mid-length, thick brown hair, and splayed, slender hands, lets out in a smooth tone.

I purse my lips. "I think evacuation of the northernmost villages is the safest option." The safety of our citizens is my top priority but, if possible, I want to try tracing their current whereabouts for leads, and I want to personally bring a more trained scouting party. Part of me cannot help but feel unstable at not being able to prevent this, but I know very well that I couldn't have; there is only now. "I plan on leading a patrol, which will leave at dawn tomorrow." I know just how pressing this moment is. My eyes settle on Driena, along with a grim smile. "Driena, you will come with me."

She nods.

I know I should choose someone to remain in my stead, and I quickly sort through the knights assembled. Soon, I settle on Turin. He is still relatively young, but he is poised and patient. His straw blonde hair clings to his forehead, eyes a deep lake blue. His firmly set chin and sweeping cheekbones add to the tattered elegance he carries with him.

"Yes, Commander." His voice resonates without hesitation, a steady look to his eyes.

Turin is capable, and I trust him in my absence. He has an excellent reading of tactics, as well as a deep concern for the citizens of Claralis. Turin is a longtime acquaintance, though I would not say we are close enough to be friends.

"I want a plan of shelter and evacuation ready in two days. It's best we notify our citizens early to the possible danger. Better for them to be nervous than cause a panic when something does happen. I want it to be addressed clearly, though make sure to reassure them. Fena, I put you in charge of organizing these plans and communicating them to the citizens."

"Of course, Liela." Fena inclines her head. Her pale, rosy red hair is set in a braid neatly over her shoulder. She has a softly freckled complexion, autumn brown eyes, and a gentle face. Her voice is soothing to hear, which makes her a presence that I know I need right now.

There's still tension in everyone's eyes, but a firm resolve too. I know I can count on the people who run this city with me. I would say I owe that to Father's rule, or maybe it is just the looming threat that preoccupies us. It eases me to know that we are a city that truly prioritizes the well-being of our citizens. Again, that is largely due to Father ... and Mother, I chide myself. Much of the city's upkeep is from her.

The Cries of a Child

Liela

I need to confront Mother. My legs feel weak at the notion, but I quickly find myself in front of her office. It stands at the far end of our family's hall—two regal-looking doors of Claralis' forest green, with an elegant silver pattern. I grasp the exquisite silver knob.

After taking a breath, I then push open the doors to Mother's office.

She sits with perfect posture, her refined elegance on full display. She wears an ankle-length midnight red dress, with a slightly low cut. A necklace centering a jade stone hangs down from her neck. Her office hosts a collection of elegant art pieces, ornate furniture with silver trimmings and cushions, and charters and treaties stamped with her seal. Her lips purse at me, and her eyes seem to command the words from my mouth.

For once, I don't hold back. "You knew about this, Mother." I'm seething, but I keep myself from yelling, my fists clenched. I deserved to know about this. I needed to know.

She looks up, startled, but quickly composes herself. "About what, Liela?" Her voice is impatient, tempered. I hate the look of her right now—sitting in a high-backed chair, like an ideal image of a queen, not just a Lord's wife. I can't see a fracture in her image.

"The attacks. You knew about them, didn't you?" My voice lowers.

She holds my gaze. "This is why I didn't tell you. You're far too quick to assume, Liela. And there's much more to this that you don't understand." She levels her gaze at me. "You're a child, and you only just became Commander. You weren't at the time of the incident with the communications. You may be my daughter, but you're shortsighted."

"What?" I stammer. "Mother!"

"I cleared up the issue to the best of my ability. I did everything I could." She looks at me, disappointed. "You could have checked the records, if you wanted to know."

"Well, I've been busy! I've had a lot going on." But a part of me feels guilty. Maybe I have enjoyed myself too much? No. I shake my head. Myllia has nothing to do with this!

"And you think I haven't?"

I silence myself at that.

She continues, "As far as I knew, the matter was resolved. I made sure to look into it personally, and tracked it to a wanted raiding group. You shouldn't have to make me say it, but there was no connection at the time to Arathulen. I can't start a war, Liela; not over something that I reasonably doubted had anything to do with a foreign party. It wasn't a pressing matter anymore, and you had every authority to access the city's files. And need I remind you that you're charged with the military. My charge is with local disputes and grievances—commerce and relations, Liela."

That really should have crossed my mind. I need to be level-headed, but my anger just won't settle.

She stares me down, and I quiver in her gaze. "Don't think I didn't take precautions—that I wasn't doing my job. I didn't raise you like that, now did I?"

"But you always looked down on me!" I yell. I know I don't make any sense, as I take a step closer to her.

"Get out," she says calmly. "You've said enough."

"What?" I feel tears in my eyes, along with a hollowness in my chest.

"Liela, I'm not coldhearted. I'm doing my best."

My knees shake, and I wipe at my eyes. "Then why didn't you tell me?"

"Because I knew you would act like a child. You always assume the worst of me."

My voice chokes up. "Then, tell me why I shouldn't!"

"Liela, I said get out." I hear aggression in her voice, and I stumble backward, like it's a blow. I know if I stay here any longer, I won't be able to hold back my tears. So, I turn, then slam the door behind me, and run down the hall to my room.

I close my door, then I collapse against it with a thud.

I furiously rub at my eyes. I'm shaking too much. I hate this! I want to scream it.

Pressing my knees to my forehead, hot tears sting at my cheeks. I need to calm down. I grip my knees tighter, hating myself for speaking up.

She's right, at least, that I'm different than her.

I don't want to judge her. I want to be able to control myself. Still, I let go a whimper into my arms.

"Can't I just do that? I'm not a child!" My voice comes out bitter, yet sometimes I feel like one. I've always felt like one in Mother's presence. I feel small and out of control. It's been that way my whole life.

My fingers loosen around my knees, and I sit slack against the door, looking at the ceiling.

Which of us is being more childish?

A Glorious Light & The Shards of Doubt

Liela

It is dawn, the light low to the horizon, reflecting almost gloriously off our armor and weapons.

I am in new riding clothes, designed specifically for my new rank—silver plating set into green, the emblem of Claralis emblazoned over my breast. I sit astride Vel, back straight and proud in the sharp, morning air. The rapier from my promotion hangs at my side. I run my hand over the hilt, feeling the increasingly familiar metal and its grounding weight.

The rest of the patrol sit astride their horses behind me, only Driena to my side.

I was busy all night preparing, and I had no time to say goodbye to Dunet or Myllia, which slits like a cruel blade at the back of my mind ... but I know Myllia has taken good care of Dunet. Her kindness stirs at my heart.

We are just inside the castle walls, grassy sprawl and uniform stone walkway leading to the castle steps at our backs, gates resting open before us to the city I must protect.

I give the signal to move out.

The weight of my position is finally settling in as I keep my head held high, despite the threat ahead of us. This is what I decided for myself, and I can think of nothing better to offer. Hopefully, this trip proves mostly uneventful, but I choose to keep an edge in my eyes, my mind sharp.

I look back once more, giving a silent goodbye to Dunet. I happen to look up, and I see Myllia on the wall, looking down at me with a distant longing in her eyes. She gives me a sweet smile that both tugs and lifts at my heart, and I give one back. I hope it carries to her. She must have found out somehow about the patrol.

With a hesitant turn of my head, I turn my eyes away from her and push myself forward.

A Trailing Sadness

Dunet

I sit in Halfern's tutoring room, late-morning light beaming through the window, dream-like and shining on the dust that catches my eyes in playful motion. Soon it only weighs on me heavier, and my heart sighs.

His office is small and orderly, lazily quiet, desk to one side set with neat compartments and a pleasant, dark-polished bookshelf, a reading armchair in one corner, and in the center of the narrow room is a window with two small, cushioned armchairs—one for each of us. And on the other side, two more windows filter in the streaming light. A door centered on the opposite side. So, it's neat, but still dusty in a bright gloom.

"Lady Dunet," comes a wise, aged voice. Halfern—his gentle blue eyes look at me from a kindly, wrinkled face, sturdy and pleasant below the quiet set of his wavy gray-brown hair.

"Yes?" I gaze up with a shake of my head.

"Do you recall what I just asked you?" His voice carries patiently, yet with a stern expectancy.

I dart my eyes away. "I'm sorry."

Halfern sighs, his gaze softening. "Lady Dunet, are you all right?"

I feel the hollow twinge of a smile, but also a tired strain. "Yes, Halfern. You can continue." My reply is half-hearted and drawn, far from the enthusiastic spark I expect from myself.

"Lady Dunet, I know this is hard for you, but you agreed to this." His eyes meet mine directly. "Just remember that you are doing this for your sister."

But it sinks past my heart, like a scorched blossom.

"Yes." I attempt to draw my mind out of its drifting. "What were we talking about?" I ask absently. My thoughts are on my sister, of course, as they always are during these sessions.

"We were talking about Mathar's civil war. Do you recall?"

"Yes," I reply, a bite to my voice. It is a piece of history I was always drawn to, but never enjoyed. It always made me feel an unpleasant turning in my stomach. A conflict surrounding three brothers, all heirs to a throne. It grates at me, especially now. Those brothers disagreed on who would take the throne and, in the end, fought for it. In a way, it mirrors something between Liela and me. I feel selfish, like I am losing her, drifting apart across a chasm like those brothers. For once, I start to understand it, if only in a different context.

As if sensing something within me, Halfern does not ask for details, and I give a quiet thank you to him. "Shall we move on?"

My lips are still dry. "Yes, I would like that." I shake myself out of my mood, trying to summon back my curiosity.

"Is there anything you would like to learn about today, Lady Dunet?"

It twists a faint smile to my face. "Florrell," I burst out. Florrell, a beautiful, lush green country, one I have always begged Liela to tell me about, even if she has never been there, because she could always weave stories like silken dreams that were so clear that I could touch them ...

Halfern turns his eyes away from me, frowning, but then he gives a satisfied smile that lights into his eyes. "There may not be much to tell about Florrell, but I am glad I found something that interests you. Very well ..."

A Short Smile

Dunet

Liela has been gone for days. She did not even say goodbye, and I feel a sinking weight creep across my eyes with each passing moment.

I stand in my honey-colored, fur boots in our field, my eyes resting on the amber disk of the horizon, my lips set tightly as I brush Eriena with my fingertips. Frost coats the stalks of grass, and the chill makes me shiver, even under my fluffy coat. I can hear the howling crackling and snapping of the wind against the stems of grass.

Eriena nuzzles me and I look absently at her. Her prodding stirs my heart into forming an affectionate smile. I reach up to scratch her behind the ears. "I have not forgotten about you."

She gives a whinny, which brings a short laugh out of me. But it isn't long before my smile falters, and I sigh, my voice laced with longing. "Why does she have to leave, Eriena?"

Eriena looks at me with sympathetic eyes, and I burrow my face into her mane, wrapping my arms around her warm, soothing neck. She paws the ground as she nuzzles back into me.

"Do you want to ride some more?" I ask. She quivers against me, and I smile peacefully, lifting out from my cloud. "I guess it will take my mind off her for a while."

I move beside her and mount, Eriena pawing at the ground once I am settled comfortably in the saddle, and it tugs warmly at my lips. I give her a pat and then signal for her to start moving. We gallop across the field, my heart beating gently, as I let the breeze bring a smile onto my face. I reach my arms out to fly on the wind, giving a joyous giggle, and I lift myself up high, frost shimmering in the morning light. Eriena runs free, and I let go a whirling laugh into that crisp, glowing air.

The Love We Need

Myllia

I don't know why, but something pulls me to Dunet's room. The guard stationed there, Grenis, acknowledges me with a nod, and I give him a kindly look back. I can feel a slight shiver through my skin, still not quite knowing what I am doing as I pass my way down the warmly lit hall towards Dunet's room.

I hesitate for a moment, in front of the door. Then, after I draw in a light breath, I give it a knock.

I hear padding footsteps, and then the door opens a crack, revealing Dunet's young, flush face that brightens in recognition. "Myllia!" She beams in the moonlight, face spreading wide as she bounces on her heels. She opens the door wider, allowing me to come in, as my left hand fiddles with my dress, out of sight of Dunet's prying eyes.

She hurries to sit on the bed, eyeing the spot beside her in a voiceless request that I sit next to her.

I give her a smile, placing all the warmth I have into it. She seemed so preoccupied at Liela's absence the other day, but I think she still had fun. Or, at least, that is what I would like to think. "How are you, Dunet?"

Her eyes cloud. "Fine."

"Are you sure?" I push with a soothing touch, but I worry all the while that I am being too straightforward.

"What is your relationship to my sister?"

It comes out small. My breath catches sharply at the unexpected question. She isn't looking at me, instead looking down at the ground, her hands clenched tightly together as her mouth sets in an unreadable crease.

"We are friends." I utterly fail at smoothness, stumbling into rosy cheeks and a quick glance at Dunet as my fingers grip at my dress.

She continues to look down mutely, a frown beginning to crease at her lips. I don't think that is what she expects me to say ... or needs me to say ...

I take a deep breath and gaze out her window at the pale moon, feeling an urge settling in my heart to be honest with Dunet. "Liela and I ... we are very close friends. I have known her for some time. She is so unique, so *Liela*." I lean into my words, as they come as easy as breathing. "Kind, caring, honest, dedicated more than anyone I have met. She is so poised, so intentional, but once you get to know her, she is so very easy to read. I find her ... well, I think her very pretty, in her own way ... She is beautiful." My heart slows to a murmur. "Liela means a lot to me, more than anyone else in my life. I don't know when exactly I realized it. I told her ..." I look back to Dunet calmly. "Well, I told her I love her. The two of us are together now. I really am happy about it, happier than I have ever been."

Dunet nods slightly, and then looks up to me with a simple, "Thank you."

I cock my head at that.

Then her smile tugs up in an irresistible gleam that shines beautifully. "I am glad ... I am glad she has you." There is such fragile honesty from her words that they catch me suddenly, my breath locking up. "You're my friend, Myllia?" She looks up, her eyes searching, as if in a final confirmation.

"Yes, of course I am."

She looks down again, her face darkening. "I was jealous of you." She gives a long, heavy pause that twists at my heartstrings. "Liela is gone so much now. I feel like I barely see her anymore." Her voice sounds so flat, so monotone, that I just want to reach for her with my breaking heart. "I saw the two of you, and I was jealous at how close you were. I don't feel the same around her and I ... I hate it."

Her voice comes out shakily, the word hate leaving her lips oddly as she scrunches her face at it, as if it feels foreign to her. She pulls her arms in closer, hands still grasping at her knees.

"I don't want things to change, because of me ... They cannot change." She gives a long pause, her breath seeming heavier, and I reach across the gap between us to squeeze her hand, her fingers trembling as they hug mine. She seems to find the words she was looking for. "I feel like I am losing her. All because I cannot accept that she is going to leave ... I cannot face that ..." Her eyes narrow through her tightening face, then she breaks all at once. Tears start to rush down her face and her chest is racked with a whimpering sob, and she presses her forehead against her knees.

I can feel the painful prickling against my own eyes as they gloss over her, wanting so much to do something for her.

"I don't want her to leave ... I want to be strong, but I can't ..." Her breath shakes. "Not like she can. I don't know how to be strong like Liela ... how to lead ... I don't want her to have to take that on too ..." Her face rests streaked with tears, and she takes a shuddering breath to slow down.

My breath comes out too fast, but I pull Dunet closer to me, to comfort her, and I let her cry, while I try desperately to sooth her ... I need to do this for Liela, help take Dunet's pain away. I barely know Dunet, but it breaks my heart to see her like this, as much as it touches me that she would even tell me. My words come out slowly as I find my voice. "Dunet, Liela loves you. She loves you more than anything; more than me, I am sure of that. The two of you have something I never will, but I'm glad."

She scrunches her face into my shoulder, and I wrap my arms around her gently, continuing with, "The fact that you feel this way means you care about Liela more than anything else." I choke on my own words. "Yes, Liela has a strength that you do not, but there is another type of strength you two still share ... love." I give her a cradling smile. "You cannot lose Liela as long as you love her, Dunet. If you don't want Liela to shoulder that burden, then take it from her, if it means that much to you." But my stomach twists, wondering if that is the right thing to say ... I utterly hope that it is. "Loving her is not selfish. I do not want to tell you to let go." I hold her tighter in emphasis. "Don't let her go. I know she will never let go of you. No matter where she is, she is thinking of you. She is too kind-hearted a person to forget. It is okay to cry ..." I try to hold my voice steady. "I really am happy that you even trust me enough to tell me this, but I want you to be happy. You still have Liela ... she will not leave you ... So, please, Dunet, spend as much time with her as you can, and enjoy it ... if for nothing else, then for me." I almost start crying myself, my voice breaking. "I will not let you go, as long as you need me. I'm here for you." I squeeze her hand. "So, please, stop blaming yourself."

Dunet sniffles as she looks at me, her eyes moist and shining, but still edged with darkness. Her smile wavers. "I'll try."

I hold onto her for minutes in silence, my own heart holding itself together with so many cracks, before Dunet pulls away, wearing a strained smile that stirs tenderly at my heartstrings. "Thank you, Myllia."

I wipe my eyes, and then I share a touching smile with her. "Of course. You can always talk to me, Dunet."

The Moments We Share

Myllia

I find myself visiting Dunet once more.

Her trust in me last night touched me deeply, probably more than she would ever realize. I want her to be happy. I can never replace Liela, but at least I can be there for her when she needs me.

I find my way up the stairs to Dunet and Liela's suite, feet gracing the steps feeling light to see her, but also so heavy, knowing what I do.

Dunet is waiting for me, her hands clasped behind her back.

She stands outside her family's suite, giving me the brightest smile I have ever seen from her, and it reduces what little preparation I had to a puddle. She is happy to see me, even if I know she is still thinking about her sister. That alone makes me smile. That look of pain and confusion ... that vulnerability she showed me the other night, is faded, but still clutched in her cheeks. I almost think something in her face looks older. Tainting new lines, but much clearer. The same joy from the market, but with a new, sorrowful sweetness.

In some ways, I really wish I had known her earlier. Although, I can't help but think that this may have never happened if I had ...

"Myllia!" She rushes over to me, catching me off guard when she throws her arms around me.

I try to form a reply, but end up simply hugging her back in answer.

I think I hear a sniffle and she looks up at me, drawing her breath in.

"I ... I needed that. Thank you again, for the other night."

My heart flutters weakly at her words of thanks, hardly needing them, and I pull up the corners of my mouth. "I want to take you somewhere today. I can't promise I will be as good of company as Liela, but I can try."

"Do you know how to ride?" Dunet squeals.

I shake my head. "No, I never learned how."

Dunet pauses with a flit to me and a cock of her head. "What do you want to do?"

"Me?" I skim for a possibility. "I would not say I have much in the way of pastimes. I think more than anything, I spend time thinking ..." My voice starts to trail absently. "I like walking in the gardens and sitting in the courtyard, and I do like visiting the markets on occasion. Nothing too exciting, I feel. I'm afraid I'm not much help. I want to do what you do, Dunet," I say to her with a cheerful, inviting smile.

"I will take you to meet Eriena!" I can see a fond light in her eyes. "After that, you can show me around the market more. I don't mind." She rises on her heels, still holding her hands behind her back. "It was fun last time! I want to know what you like!" Her curiosity touches my heart.

I tilt my head warmly towards her. "Then, we can go to the market."

Dunet grabs my hand, running me to the stairs. We make our way through the castle and out to the stables in the gleaming sunshine. I pick up the hem of my dress, unprepared. I really rarely run. I am unaccustomed to it, but there's such a twinkling in Dunet's eyes that I cannot disappoint her.

We reach the stables, and I am out of breath. I bend over to pant, breathing in the fresh, dewy air.

Dunet is full of energy, still. It seems limitless.

"I think you really need Liela for this," I say, still panting. An image pops into my head of Liela running, pulling a wistful smile onto my face that sweeps in a tickle over my skin. Beads of sweat run down my neck. "I really hope I do not ruin my dress." I look down in a frown, sinking against the wall of the stable.

"Are you okay, Myllia?" She looks at me, her forehead creased.

"Yes." I breathe out in a daze. "Just tired."

She cocks her head innocently. It looks cute. Then it seems to dawn on her, as her eyes glance wide and she murmurs, "Sorry."

"No." I laugh. "It was rather fun. I just never do anything like this."

She looks at me more, brow still furrowed, before turning her eyes away and bounding into the stables, resting silently in the morning shadows cast in a lazy haze. She comes back a moment later, leading a horse I assume to be hers. "This is Eriena!" Dunet beams, looking lovingly at the horse.

"She looks beautiful." I reach my hand up to pet her, as Eriena leans forward into my touch.

"You still don't want to try riding?" Dunet's voice twitches up.

"I really do not think I could," I say with a frown. "Thank you, though." I smile weakly. I know I would probably fall as soon as I got in the saddle.

"I could teach you sometime, though I'm still learning." She glances back at Eriena. "Liela could show you much better."

"Thank you. I will think on it."

"I want you to show me around the market!"

"Of course!"

"Can you pick out a dress for me, like you did for Liela?" She rocks on her feet. Her eyes twinkle expectantly.

I feel a burning at my ears as I remember how beautiful Liela looked. I brush the image aside, smiling sweetly at Dunet. "Of course, I can."

I come back inside the stable as Dunet leads Eriena in, patting at her mane and whispering, "I will be back to see you soon," before she turns to me and bounds over.

We step outside. This time, she takes my hand and leads me, in a walk, to the market down the thoroughfare. Her thoughtfulness warms my heart. I look to the side and give her a warm smile, and she responds with a beaming one of her own.

We reach the market, sun glaring over the streets.

Dunet has held my hand the whole way here, and I cling to it in softness, her warmth and innocent spirit filling me with joy. She seems to be herself again, after our talk. Or, at least, the sister Liela talked about.

The market sprawls out before us, rich bits of color mixing all the brighter in the late fall sunlight, over masses of people flowing leisurely past the stalls. Despite the cold, the market seems just as lively, feet mixing against the sprawl of dirt, sweet smells hitting my nostrils all at once.

I think everyone is so used to Claralis' cold that it's hardly a bother, with everyone bundled so snuggly, me with my white and violet fur coat over a bright yellow dress, touched with warmth by the sun. It is my favorite color, yellow, but ever since telling Liela that it was, I find myself unconsciously selecting it more than I normally would. Dunet has a longer, black coat this time, with dapper buttons. She wears it over her white flowing dress and honey, fur-lined boots, hands slipped into gray-white mittens.

We move through the stalls and the shops lining the buildings, my hand carefully holding Dunet's. I stop to glance at a few: a merchant selling beautiful, vivid dyes, a fabric shop with velvet that is so silky smooth that I hesitate in not buying any, but I do want to set a good example by not spending recklessly. We also pass a stall selling delicious-looking, fresh pastries.

Dunet pulls at me, and I turn my steps to follow her, warmth flecking my eyes.

"Anything I can get you young ladies?" A kindly looking woman with wispy, white hair, wrinkles, clear blues eyes, and a beautiful smile offers us from behind a wooden cart with a white cloth over the tabletop, overhung with a light gold and ruby tapestry of a brilliant weave, shading out the sun.

Dunet stares at the case to the side of the counter and points at a particularly good-looking pastry, stuffed with a sweet blackberry filling that seeps through the air. The woman pulls it from the case with delicate fingers. She hands it to Dunet's eager hands as I ruffle through my purse for coins, which I hand to her.

"Thank you, dears. Have a wonderful day shopping."

I smile back at her. "We will, and thank you."

I step over to a nearby table-top, motioning for Dunet to join me.

She skips over to the opposite seat at the white-twined table with a glass tabletop and overhanging pink umbrella, eating and gazing at the passers-by in a lazy current.

Dunet nibbles through it in a frenzy and then licks at her fingers in delight, which makes me laugh.

"I think you enjoyed that twice as much as I did." I gently rest my eyes on her.

She looks up, a finger still dangling in her mouth, and she grins at me with a giggle. Swiping her finger out, she says, "Thank you, Myllia! I love blackberries! They're so delicious!"

I look away quickly, slipping into an, "Of course."

Dunet sinks back into her chair, casting her eyes up. "Myllia ..." She sighs, her eyes flitting quickly as she holds onto her smile. "I think ... No." She shakes her head. "I'm sorry that I'm still pretending."

It jolts through me just how quickly her expression falls and my heart sinks. "Dunet?"

She smiles in a faded glow. "But, let me. Thank you, Myllia. I need to try, but I want you to know more than anyone that I am pretending ... if only you ..."

"Thank you, but you do not have to pretend for me."

She squirms. "But I want to, or else I don't know what to do or say." Her eyes stare back behind me, at the castle.

"Just be you ..." I breathe consolingly.

She shakes her head, tracing a mournful smile. "Myllia, can I tell you something?"

I shift the full weight of my eyes to her. "Of course, you can, Dunet."

"Well, I feel lonely half the time. I don't know how to talk to people, or be anyone other than what everyone else sees. I want something more." Her breath falls. "But it makes me scared. I just want to make people happy." Her eyes turn desolate in that moment. "I can barely talk to anyone other than Liela, and no one besides you like this ... because I don't know what to do. It makes me feel like I'm drowning."

"Dunet, I think people want to see more of who you are."

"No, they don't." She meets my eyes directly, as I've rarely seen her do, then pulls on a smile and looks away. "Don't tell Liela about this, please."

"I won't, but I think you should, Dunet."

She shakes her head again. "I'm okay if I feel lonely ..."

I start reaching across the table. "That is not okay, Dunet ... to be alone, so don't say that."

Her lip quivers and she takes my hand, before drawing it back suddenly. "Thank you, Myllia."

I just smile tenderly. "Anything you need from me, Dunet; I want to make you smile."

Her smile falters and turns dark. She raises her shoulders and pulls it on more brilliantly. "I want you to take me around some more!" She jumps to her feet, glancing around in a rekindled, but furtive spark, and I rise delicately to follow, nearly reaching for her to stop and slow down, because I am not sure that ignoring her problems is what she wants. I think all she wants, and needs, is to talk, but I don't have the heart to force her to do so.

~

I buy her a crimson scarf to wear, with the increasingly cold weather in mind. I almost laugh at how much cuter it makes her look, making her cheeks glow, setting into her sapphire eyes, and lighting against her buttery hair and white dress.

At last, after that little purchase, I bring her back to the dress shop, pushing open the door to the musty, magical maze of racks. I let Dunet roam and bound her way around the room, while I go to select a dress, running my hands in thought over the fabrics.

I want it to be perfect. White really does suit her, but I think she has plenty of it.

My eyes settle on a dress that I think would look good on her, cherry red and simple.

I call to Dunet, and she comes running on light feet. Her eyes focusing on the dress, sparkling.

"Does this seem like something you'd like?" I peek at her.

"Yes!" she says, swiveling from side-to-side. "I love it!"

"Do you want to try it on?"

She looks questioningly for a moment between me and the dress, as I hand it to her, then takes it and heads into the changing room. I let my eyes play pleasantly over the bright colors of the racks, my heart still aching for Dunet, but all the while, I feel a warm rush at the fuzzy moment.

She emerges shortly after with the dress on, and I give a satisfied smile at the result. It fits her well, highlighting her youthful, innocent side, while making the color on her cheeks appear more vivid.

Dunet looks down at herself and gives a twirl, arms extended outwards with a giggle, and then she twines her hands behind her back as her large eyes find me again.

"You look lovely, Dunet."

I do consider, though, does this color *really* suit her?

"Can I have you try on another?"

Dunet gives another simple, bright "Yes!" and I pull away to search for another, while she follows me with curious eyes. "Myllia, what makes you like dresses?"

I pose my mouth thoughtfully. "They make me feel pretty and beautiful and free, like in a fairytale. I feel alive. Plus, I was always so romantic. They feel *me*." My thoughts turn to Liela. "You know, Dunet, I always daydreamed of distant places. I love storybooks and romance, so Liela is my dream, you might say ..." I trail off wistfully. "All I ever wanted is now in her."

She nods. "I'm glad that you're with my sister." She meets my eyes with a genuine light. "I'm happy I met you."

My heart melts tenderly at her kind words. "I guess I was a little worried, so I was hoping you would say that." I break into a breeze of a laugh.

Dunet smiles wonderfully, tapping her toe against the floor. "I was afraid you'd think otherwise."

"And I'm glad you reassured me. You know, Dunet ..." My eyes sparkle. "We'll have the most wonderful wedding! I can see it in my eyes. Well, I guess I was planning it for a while. I was thinking that you could be the flower girl."

Her eyes twinkle. "Really?"

"Yes, though I know I have to wait quite a while, so as not to shock Liela. I can jump to things I want very quickly."

She giggles as she stares up at me.

Well, of course, I am planning a little too far out, but I have it set in my mind.

I turn my eyes back to the racks, eyes lingering on a violet dress, and I pry it from the rack, holding it up in front of Dunet to give myself a sense of its fit and look. "Will you try this one on?" I press the fabric into her reaching palms.

She rushes back to the dressing room, ducking in, a blossoming smile still on my lips.

She comes out with a skip.

My eyes settle in wonder over her small frame. "You do look beautiful, Dunet." The dress seems to perfectly capture her joy and youth, while hinting at the cusp of maturity.

"Which one do you like better?" she presses.

Thinking the question over, I know which one suits her more at this moment. "The purple one, I would say, though I think I will buy them both, if you like them."

"I do!" Her voice rings, bright and high.

Perhaps I am treating her too much, but I really am enjoying spending time with Dunet. It feels refreshing and new.

She steps a-rhythmically at my side as we move to the counter. A dark-haired, gorgeous woman with pale-blue eyes, a slender frame, mature smile, and an elegant, sensual dress stands there looking off to the side. "Alice!" I call lightly.

She leans forward over the counter. "Anything you found? I see you brought a beautiful girl."

"My name is Dunet!" Dunet bursts out, before looking down.

Alice turns to me with a sumptuous smile.

"Just a dress for her," I say smoothly, then look back at Dunet's still downturned eyes. "Actually, two."

She looks up at me, her eyes widening as I hand over the dresses and pay. I convince myself that I can buy her two dresses and a scarf as a treat. I probably would have done the same for myself.

Alice draws up and smiles sweetly as we turn away.

Afterwards, we visit the sweet shop again, saying hello to Helin once more, who is thrilled to see us both. I convince myself I am too full to indulge myself further. I catch Helin sneaking another piece of candy to Dunet. She has found a new favorite.

"Come back any time!" She smiles from under her pixie hair that draws my eyes, as she leans back against the counter.

We exit the shop, Dunet's feet dragging, and I hail a carriage. The sun is already setting low in a crimson gold across the horizon, stars beginning to peek out, as I grace the steps to the polished wood carriage set with gold trim, sinking into the red, plush cushions. Dunet drowses against my shoulder, murmuring weakly, "Thank you, Myllia." She scrunches at her eyes, giving a small yawn. "That was fun ..."

I tuck my head back, my own eyelids heavy. "I had fun too."

She seems weightless and nearly happy right now. Maybe I made her forget about Liela, I think, before it turns to guilt that I hope doesn't show on my face. Fortunately, Dunet doesn't seem to notice. As we bump along, nearing the castle, I see a flicker of longing cross her face. She grows even quieter as she looks ahead, gazing out the window specked with stars.

I hold her hand as we cross the ground sleepily, her eyes dull in exhaustion, feet dragging up the stairs. I wish I was strong enough to carry her.

By the time we pass through the warm hallway of the suite and into her room in moonbeams and starlight, she collapses on her bed.

I tuck her in carefully, before exiting the room, closing the door softly behind me.

A Glancing Daydream

Myllia

An unsettling feeling creeps into my consciousness with greater frequency, the closer I get to Dunet. Liela isn't back yet and my chest aches. I feel like I am taking Dunet away from her. It rips at me that my words may not be enough to comfort Dunet. She is strong, but I can tell she is dwelling on her sister's absence far more than she must.

I sigh, gazing at the pond in the courtyard; it brings many fond, dreamy memories of Liela and me to my mind. This pond let me learn her bit by bit, until I was falling into her and knew without a doubt what I wanted.

My breath comes out in a cloud of mist. A dusting of snow coats the ground, still thin and powdery, barely covering the grass and flowers. It is twilight, a serene nature falling on the courtyard. I look up, the occasional snowflake filtering through the boughs of the tree above me.

I lean back against the tree. My thoughts still drift to Liela. I yearn for her to be here again, and to feel the touch of her holding me here. I put a hand to my lips, feeling where she kissed me not so long ago. I want to feel those rippling goosebumps on my skin; I want to dance with her again ... to be held in her slender arms and the sharpness of her soft eyes, or to simply sit beside the pond and talk ...

Without realizing it, I drift off, caught in my thoughts, spinning them into the dreamy twilight as the atmosphere envelops me in misty silence.

Lingering Doubts

Liela

I dismount from Vel, feet crunching on the splintered wood and slick mud, my eyes hard on the grim sight of the village—it's set in scorched splinters and toppled beams of what were once houses. I turn away as bile rises in my throat, my eyes stinging at the sight of those dead families, burned from their peace. But I bring my eyes back, taking deep breaths through the freezing sheet of rain. It still brings revulsion, but I need to see it, if only to strengthen my conviction.

We have been riding and setting camp for nearly a week. My muscles are sore from the days on the road. Whoever we are tracking, we have seen hardly a trace, and we have found nothing to identify them or their numbers with certainty.

But one thing is certain: their tracks cross back over the border into Arathulen. My teeth grind over my lip as I clench my fist, mind failing me in a cold dread.

And we dare not follow too far over the border. I have no desire to initiate a dispute or a war, and break our fragile peace treaty. I know that Arathulen can be unpredictable.

Fortunately, I can rest somewhat at ease knowing that most of the villages have been evacuated to Claralis. There should be a steady stream of the dispossessed by now. It brings desperate tears from my eyes to see them, but I stand tall nonetheless, offering a comforting hand when I can.

It's a relief that only one village has been attacked so far under our jurisdiction.

I shouldn't have blamed Mother for this ... It's a sober realization, and one I can't afford to dwell on.

I walk through the heavy silence of those knights carrying the dead to a burial, eyes shutting for a passing moment, and then I go through to the tents and into the rising sheets of the command tent, staked in the center. I brush the flaps aside and move toward the shivering flames of candles, rain beating overhead, table in the center with a pinned map laid out with evacuation plans, several quills, and reports brought by couriers. A few chairs are set around the table.

Driena brings her eyes up to me and gives a solemn nod that I return in kind.

I turn to Lendis—his normally easy face is now lined, ashy brown hair disheveled from the road, and his hands rest tiredly at his sides. "Have a message sent to Siltheus, Lendis. Their patterns are too efficient to be a mere raiding party. We will need reinforcements." I keep my voice steady. I am much more concerned than I let on, but I want everyone calm.

"Yes, Commander." He inclines his head and turns away.

The other knights in the tent ruffle over plans with weary eyes.

Driena draws herself up and walks over to me. "Want to go outside, Liela?"

I only nod with that same weariness, as we push out into the icy rain.

My gaze once again returns to that grim scene in front of me, my lips pursed.

Driena gives me a look that grounds me. "There isn't much more we can do, is there?"

"I know there isn't."

"Liela, we will push through this." Her lips are tight, her eyes resolute.

"I will believe that for as long as we can. And I know I couldn't have done more, but it is still hard to see."

"I know it is, Liela."

I sigh. "I know it's time that I resume my command in the city. As much as I want to help with evacuations, my place is not here."

"And that is why I know how much you care, Liela. So, I know"—she meets my eyes directly in a promise—"that we will not fail our people. You were never one who could do that."

"Neither are you, Driena."

"That is why I am grateful. I think you know what you must do, and I will always follow you. For once ... I really understand how much responsibility I now have, and I know it can and will be crushing, but we will hold each other up. Liela, you were always like my sister." Her eyes gloss over as she smiles at me. "And I know I have one, but you're like an *older* sister."

"And I would say the same, if not for Dunet."

"I know you would. You are stubbornly kind, in that way." Her eyes lessen in their intensity.

I make up my mind: we are to depart, falling back to Claralis to form a defensive position, while leaving several trusted knights to finish up the remains of the evacuation. We can rely on scouts from here on out. I want our forces collected and ready for an assault in Claralis. Moving everyone leaves them vulnerable, but I need to chance it, because behind Claralis' walls is the safest place right now, until we receive aid.

I turn resolutely, aware of Driena's grounding presence still at my side, and I give the order to move out. Then we strike out, away, leaving the burnt village at our backs.

A Quiet Dawn

Dunet

I stare out the window as the midmorning sunlight pops off the newly settled snow. The city sounds silent, like it is sleeping peacefully.

A gust of crisp wind ripples over my hair, and I watch it flutter in the breeze with absent eyes.

I feel a slight pang as I lean out farther. I have found myself growing increasingly lonely, flailing quietly into a chasm that consumes me. Maybe that feeling was always there, but if I had Liela, I knew I could ignore it.

And now, my chest is building dangerously, and my eyes fall away from places I would rather not look. I don't want to feel this.

The world always felt small and alive with Liela. Nothing was ever dull. She was always there for me ... solely for me.

Maybe I never thought a day would come when I would have to choose between two things I never wanted.

I force myself to smile again, even as it strains painfully at those dimples that never seem to go away.

Sometimes I just feel tired.

I feel like I should not, though, and I find myself wanting to just press through it.

Shaking my head, I lie my forearms over the snow-laden windowsill.

I feel a slight dryness in my throat, as I let a tear slides down my face.

"I don't want this," I whisper, a low scorching to my words. I stare out at the city, a bittersweet smile crossing my face as I think of Myllia comforting me.

I like her. She makes me feel safe.

But I feel guilty for placing so much on her that I would never share with my sister.

Maybe ...?

I don't know how to give this feeling words ... like a building of nothingness.

Closing my eyes for a moment and blinking back the tears, I breathe deeply and lean forward onto my toes. Myllia said she wanted me to be happy for her, if for nothing else, so I pull a fragile smile to my face. I can at least do that, right? Maybe everything will be all right, even if it hurts?

"For Liela," I sigh out.

Then I let my mind wander, wondering where she is, what she is doing right now ... and if she is thinking about me.

Tears of Innocence

Dunet

Liela is back.

Her patrol comes through the gates, uninjured, and shaky relief fills my mind. I see Liela at the head of the column, conversing with one of her knights, expression dour and taut, but my heart feels so full.

Myllia is with me, holding onto my hand and looking at Liela with a swirl in her eyes.

My feet rise giddily as the patrol trots closer. It takes me a second to realize it, but my heart is pounding. Why should I be nervous? It's Liela, my sister.

Myllia squeezes my hand, as if she senses my nervousness.

When the patrol is close enough, I run up to her with a winged cry. "Liela!"

Her gaze moves to me. It seems distant, and for a moment I don't see that recognition and light I look for in her eyes—drawn and tired, they gaze past me for a mere moment.

My blood runs cold, and I am frozen there.

Then her face softens, bringing with it that familiar warmth, but it fails to break the ice on my feet. I drag my lips into a smile, but I don't move closer. Liela gives me an apologetic smile, as if saying that she will see me later. The rest of the patrol, along with Liela, moves by, while I'm rooted to the spot.

Someone comes up beside me and I realize it is Myllia. "Dunet ..." She turns her eyes to me—they seem to knock at the door of my heart, but I am not there to answer her . My mind is hazy. "Dunet, are you okay?" She reaches for me, but before she can comfort me, I turn, sprinting away from her.

I desperately scratch at my eyes, which sting under their wall of watery mist, blinding me.

Liela? She ... My mind tosses, reaching for something to hold onto. That look flashes clearly against my eyelids. I find it hard to breathe through the grip in my chest. It hurts so much.

I close my eyes, but all I can see is her gazing at me, not seeing me. I stumble and fall, but I don't care through this numbness. Absently, I hear Myllia running after me, panting. I push myself up and keep running. I don't know where to go. I just run.

I end up in the stables.

"Dunet!"

I ignore that call, which rings cruelly in my heart. It's something I want to turn away from, as much as I may need it.

Eriena gazes at me with sorrowful eyes, as she sees my streaking tears. I open her stable door and then collapse into the dirt and hay, body wracking violently as I clutch and scrape my nails at the dirt underneath. Eriena nuzzles me, but I don't respond.

Several seconds later, I hear light footfalls, and then the creak of Eriena's stable gate.

I wish I could hide and disappear far away from here ... then no one would have to see me. But my mind is too heavy to move.

I feel a brush of air, and then Myllia is sitting beside me. "Dunet—" Her voice catches.

"Did you see how she looked at me, Myllia? It was like she didn't know me." My voice escapes me bitterly.

There's a short silence. I hear Myllia's breath pick up. "She did not mean it ... you *know* she didn't." And I can tell that those are not quite the words she is looking for—she sounds mechanical in my ears.

"But she did," I choke, my throat throbbing.

Myllia lays a hand on me in comfort. "There probably is nothing that I can say to make it hurt less. Liela never wanted to hurt you." She breathes in. "Whatever situation she is in, it is probably putting her under a lot of stress. She loves you." Myllia sighs. "I am sure that look was not meant for you."

It rings true, but it still stings unbearably. "I know that." I can barely control the shakiness in my voice. "But it still hurts." I finally bring myself to look up at Myllia.

"I know ..." Her voice breaks like glass.

She brings me into an embrace, holding me tightly. I bury myself in her. "I just need time ..."

She doesn't reply, though her chest shakes, only holding me tighter.

I bite down on my lip, letting my tears stream in silence. Finally, I pull away, eyes glistening. I reach to wipe them away with a trembling hand.

I look back up to Myllia, dress stained with dirt, mud, and my tears, as well as her own. I shudder. "Myllia, your dress ..."

She looks down at it in puzzlement, then gives me a soft smile, lips quivering up beautifully, so much care and compassion behind them. "That doesn't matter to me now. I know, I look horrible. Please do not tell Liela." Her cheeks turn to a shy blush.

I give a genuine laugh, feeling immense gratitude, which I want her to see in my eyes.

"Will you take me riding?" she asks. "At least, I can say I am more appropriately dressed now."

I feel a little stunned, a giggle escaping me. "Yes! I ... I would love to!"

With the help of one of the stable hands—a quiet girl with brown braided hair, Illis—I pick out a horse for Myllia. Her name is Ina. She is polite and sweet, and I think she is perfect for Myllia.

"Ina." Myllia talks soothingly. "That is a nice name." She leads Ina out of the stable into the lacing gold-orange glow of the mountains, the sky above still a pale blue. She strokes her after we move through the gates, to the shorter grass bordering the edge of the field. "You are a good girl, Ina."

I show a small smile, confident enough in my riding now to help her. "Can you mount her?"

Myllia's gaze turns quizzical. She really has never done this before, and it twitches at my smile. "I can try." Clumsily, she attempts to mount, and I suppress a giggle as I bend over, eyes bright with tears.

Liela

I finish the meeting, striding from the room, even as my steps threaten to falter.

Guilt has been working at the back of my mind from the moment I passed Dunet and Myllia, and now it comes in full force. She seemed to stop moving when I looked at her. It puzzles me, but more than that, I thought I caught something else in her expression. Why, though?

I go to find her. I can push her to the back of my thoughts during the meeting, but now, more than anything, I want to see her and Myllia.

I stop quickly by her room. Not seeing her, I go to the courtyard for Myllia. When I don't find either of them, it settles in me that they must be at the stables, or nearby in the field. Maybe I knew that, but I was just trying to drag along the time? I feel dread to seeing her ... almost ominous.

Myllia greets me as she is ... trying to mount a horse. A laugh escapes. "Do you need help, Myllia?"

She turns, cheeks red, and a thrill rocks my heart. Her dress is stained with dirt, I notice. She then turns her gaze with a flicker to Dunet and I see something pass between them that aches at my heart.

I look to Myllia with a question. Maybe I am even jealous that I don't understand what is going on between them, but I drop that thought as quickly as I can, because I want to be happy that they have something. Why am I thinking that, though? I left her to sit in a council chamber for an hour. Why should they wait for me?

I turn my gaze to Dunet. She looks down, but not before I see the torn shadow in her eyes.

"Dunet?" My voice wavers, reaching for her.

She stands there silently. Time stretches, my lips dry. She turns away, hiding her face. "I ..." I notice her voice trembling. "I need some time alone."

Something shatters in my chest, and I lose my voice.

"Dunet?" I call out again, my voice breaking.

She holds still and then runs in the other direction.

I desperately follow, but Myllia's kind face stops me, heavy and wavering. "Liela ..." She is caught between us, fiddling with her dress, before she looks directly at me with a gentleness and my heart stops. "I think you should let her be alone for a while." Her words are quiet, trailing off at the end.

"Myllia?" My eyes cloud on her.

She sighs. "She ... she needs time."

"What happened, Myllia?" I ask, my legs threatening to buckle. I dread her response.

"It ... the way you looked at her today ... well, she took it the wrong way, and it hurt her. She's confused."

I think back. "The way I looked at her?" It dawns on me then and my mind fills with cold regret, a chill falling over me. I wish I could reach back to that moment. I was too lost in thought and exhaustion over the situation, that it took me a second to process that Dunet was there. That was why she stopped, how I hurt her ... My mind recoils harshly from that truth. "Myllia ..." My voice is broken. "What should I do?" I feel helpless and lost, turning to Myllia for support, but I don't know what to do except that ... because I need her now.

I avoid her gaze, heart fading in a low cry. The next moment, she is hugging me, voice so soothingly kind in my ear. "I know you did not mean it. I wish I could tell you what to do, but to be truthful, I am completely at a loss. Give her time." For me, she holds herself together. "She already realizes, but she is still young and confused. If she does not come to you, then go see her."

Myllia

My words feel hollow, they feel wrong.

She holds onto me, as if to anchor herself. Her breathing is uneven and her grip on me seems much too hard, yet she is weak and shaking with uncertainty.

"If you need to cry, cry," I murmur softly in her ear, the only kindness I can give.

She nods slowly, biting her lip. I feel her composure breaking. Then it collapses, and she releases a sob, opening up to me, fully vulnerable. She is like a child, finally letting her emotions run free, and I clutch her closer.

Liela

Everything rushes out like a flood. Myllia holds me, comforts me, and I let her.

What is happening? Dunet is changing—she is growing up, all because I forced her to. It feels too soon, too cruel. I feel like I'm suffocating. I never thought I would lose her, not this young, not ever.

My mind reels with unbearable loss, and I give a strangled shriek, still clinging to Myllia, my head bent over her shoulder.

All my fault, all my fault, all my fault ...

The words repeat over and over again. My pride, honor, dignity, poised confidence, what is it if I don't have Dunet?

I sink into Myllia, still shaking violently as my mouth opens wide in a silent shriek, tears piling in my eyes and drowning me.

"It isn't your fault, Liela." Myllia strokes my hair as I weep, and I cling to her words.

I realize my nails are digging into her back, and soften my grip. I pant, mind still roiling; my world seems to crumble, and my body is wracked in so many silent screams, as my eyes pinch in their tears. Finally, I go still, my breath growing more even.

"Just be there for her, Liela. She still needs you. She ... both of you have a lot to think about right now." Her voice is a patient stroke.

I nod, my lips set, to stop from trembling. Tears still run down my cheeks. I stay like that for another minute, needing her warmth, before removing myself from her.

"I do not like to see you like that, Liela ... or Dunet. I do not like to think it, but you are beautiful when you cry."

I give a strained smile, my heart breaking once more and simultaneously melting.

"She will come back to you. You will just have to be there for her. She was always going to grow up and you have to grow with her. It's hard, but this was going to happen eventually. She wants to rule for you, and you have the army. You two just have to realize that and grow closer. You are a good sister, Liela," she adds simply, eyes bright and kind.

"Thank you, Myllia. I feel better, even if it still makes me sad." The weight of it all feels crushing, but Myllia makes it light enough to hold.

Myllia lets me think in silence for a bit.

What should I have done differently? I don't even know how to support her now.

I try to clear my head, but the truth is I feared this more than anything.

I keep finding myself looking to Myllia, like she has the answers. Will I really let Dunet take up the burden of leading Claralis? Can I bear seeing her become Lord?

Can I even bear her to see grow up?

I was always so stubborn. In this moment, I feel like I know so little. I only know how to be one thing for her.

But, I never really knew her ... I only knew what I wanted to know. And that realization is a cold one.

She struggled, but I tried so hard not to notice. I did the one thing I never wanted to do.

I hurt her. I wanted to shelter her forever.

I squeeze my eyes shut, and see that pain in her eyes.

I can't think about this right now. All I know is that I did something wrong somewhere. I know that I have to help her somehow, but I don't know how.

How could I really be a good sister? I wouldn't believe that I was a good sister at all, if Myllia hadn't said it. I want to believe everything she says ... because I love her.

I look pleadingly up at Myllia, and she seems to read my expression, knowing that I need a distraction.

"Would you like to show me how to ride?" she asks gently. Her eyes meet mine playfully, as if to take my mind off my brokenness.

I look at her, a bit distantly.

"I really am terrible at it." She giggles with a tender smile.

At that, she gets through to me, and I break into a laugh, thinking back to her attempt at mounting that I arrived just in time to witness.

"Plus, I want to be able to ride with Dunet ... and you." Her eyes cradle me.

"I will." The shakiness dissipates a fraction from my voice.

Myllia

Liela finally gets me to mount, though with some help. Heat crawls into my cheeks.

I do a few short trots, circles, and short lines, heart wavering dangerously as I swing precariously in the saddle.

"I want you to dismount," Liela calls to me.

"I cannot," my voice wavers, heart wrenching as I try to swing my leg over the saddle.

Liela comes over to me. "I will be right here," she says reassuringly. I look deeply into her eyes, which wait for me.

I start to fall, and Liela catches me in her arms. I look up at her and she gives me a tender, loving smile, still fragile from emotion. Heat swells in my cheeks and goosebumps blossom over my skin as she holds me delicately. It feels so romantic, her arms wrapped beneath me, holding me against her, and I move to kiss her. She returns it.

Maybe I shouldn't be indulging myself now, but I can't help wanting to. And maybe it is just to delay everything, but I want to keep Liela's mind off her sister while I can.

Dunet

The urge to scream left me an eternity ago, the last biting tears drying on my cold cheeks. But that crushing feeling remains, making it hard to breathe. I dig my fingernails into my arm until it bleeds, my lips still wobbling.

I hide my arm as I look up.

Eriena has followed me, and I stroke her numbly. "I'm so sorry, Eriena." My voice breaks hollowly. I am grateful for her, for I would truly suffocate without her.

There's no reason for me to feel such coldness, but I struggle not to. I need to tell her I lover her, and that I'll be Lord. I need to apologize for hurting her. Yet, I can't see myself doing any of these things. But not saying anything would be selfish. How could I possibly deserve to be Lord? I know I'm not even good enough for Liela. I only want to be Lord to make her forgive me ... I'll apologize to her for running, because I can't bear anything else. I need her, and I love her. Without her, I'm alone, and I don't know who I am without her.

I shouldn't have run away from her, but I couldn't stay there. I ran without thinking. And now, I want to do anything but see her.

I know I want to apologize, but it's agonizing to even move.

I bring my eyes up in a selfish whisper. "Help me, Eriena ..."

She pushes closer to me. I grasp her mane as she pulls herself up, so heartbreakingly gentle.

I sniffle and wipe at my running nose. "Thank you, Eriena. You are too good for me."

With a shaky breath in, I draw up my shoulders and look straight, knowing what I have to do ... that I have to see her ...

It would be far too selfish not to, and I take a step forward, Eriena following me to the edge of the field and giving me the strength to push forward and face her after I broke her.

Liela

Dunet is still in my mind, and I start turning my eyes in the direction of the stables behind the wall, dusk a faint, golden gray-blue as torches and lanterns start lighting along the wall. It has been almost an hour since she left, and my skin is prickling.

Myllia finishes her practice, lying on the grass in apparent exhaustion, a smile playing softly on her lips, eyes closed. I move to sit next to her, and she sits up, hugging her knees and casting her cornflower gaze thoughtfully to me. I look off into the distance, wondering where she is and if she is all right.

Minutes of silence go by, as fireflies start flitting through the stalks of grass. My heart floats numbly with them, and I finally see her, my heart twisting before it falls into a grateful warmth. I stand as she walks towards us, looking down, her eyes in shadow. A pang of loss hits me. She stops a short distance from me. Her eyes are dry, but I see streaks of tears coating her cheeks.

The words leave me slowly, but they're meaningful. "Dunet, I am so sorry." I cannot think of what else to say.

She looks up, and seeming to see something in my face, she runs towards me, flinging her arms around me. "I love you, Liela." Her face buries into me with the hot release of tears.

"I love you too, Dunet. I ... I won't let you go. I am sorry I'm so busy, and sorry I looked at you that way ... I wish it were different, but ..."

Her words are clear and quiet. "It's okay. I think I knew, but ... I don't want to accept it. I will, though." She looks up, her eyes burning steadily. "I have decided ... I will be Lord." Her voice is so resolute that it and halts my breath; all the doubt is gone from her voice.

Then, it hits me. She really is growing up. "You don't have to." I don't want her to, especially not for my sake.

"I will." And I see a firm spark in her eyes.

I don't know what to say—my voice trembles. "I will always be here for you, Dunet."

"I know," she says, like she has always understood, and my chest seems to mend and break at the same time. This is still Dunet, I tell myself.

"I love you," I repeat in a whisper.

I'd do anything for her.

Even if it costs me everything.

If I had to pick her above all, I would. Wouldn't I?

Because I love her more than anything.

And so,

If you forget I love you,

I'll be there to tell you I do.

~ End of Part 1 ~

Caroline Sophia Hamel

Caroline Sophia Hamel

Acknowledgments

First of all, I have to thank all of my test readers. This book would be nowhere close to where it is without you, and I learned so much by taking the time to be patient, listen, and let everything sink in, so that I could learn from you. Elena Irish, you were my first test reader, and you showed so much interest in and patience for my book. That means a lot to me, that you took the time to read this. The book has changed so much since then, and I hope you like it.

I need to thank my mom for seeing my book for what it is and being the first person to tell me that it was beautiful. Those were the words that stuck with me and what I wanted others to see in my writing. Much of this book wouldn't exist without you in my life. In a way, this book is for us.

I want to thank Katherine Atkins for helping me push past my fears and insecurities I had with showing people my work, and learn to push forward to better myself with the things I love and to put more effort into something I know I care so much about and to never give up on it ... You pushed me to write drafts 2 and 3, and to bring the book to where it is now.

To Luke Shealy, who was so kind in the utter extent of feedback you gave me, going out of your way to help me with something you knew I treasured to my heart ... I'm still simply astounded at your 10,000+ words of feedback, given to me selflessly. You really let me dive fully into this world and my characters with the desires you expressed in wanting to know more about them and their world, and how you wanted to see things through their eyes more clearly, so that you could understand them and my book to its fullest. You've helped this book be something that can reach more people. You encouraged me to write draft 4 ... and to rewrite my entire book in draft 5. I was able to stretch less than 50 pages from my earlier drafts into a lush and sprawling book that is 100 times better, because you encouraged me to slow down and feel and think about every word that I put to the page.

To Konoha Tomono Duval, who showed me that I was still telling my emotions, rather than showing them. You helped my writing blossom in a way it never could before, encouraging me to write draft 6. This book would not touch as deeply without your support.

I want to thank Rob and Kathy Holman and Allison Hamel for showing interest in my book and being early readers. I also appreciate everyone's support at my workplace.

I want to thank everyone at Village Books who helped me get through many of the stages of the self-publishing process. I am beyond grateful for the self-publishing service you offered, which made it much easier to self-publish. I especially want to thank Rachel Johnson, for just giving me this opportunity, believing in my book, and helping me with so many of my questions. Also, thank you to Chloe Hovind and Chelanne Evans, who answered many of my other questions after Rachel left, and helping me sort through delays and printer errors. Thank you for your patience.

I want to thank my beta reader, Paige Downey (paigedown) on Fiverr, for her clear communication, detailed feedback, clarifications, and thoughtful suggestions. You helped with my uncertainty on whether the middle sections of my book worked the way I wanted them to. I would highly recommend her, especially for LGBTQ+ books (@paiges.bookstore on Instagram)!

I want to thank everyone in my social media, advertising, and publishing course for writers: the Writer's Coffee Lounge, hosted by Sadie Faith Anderson, who I thank for all the resources you provided us. This course has also given me so many connections to a community of authors and poets that I am really grateful for.

I want to thank Ethan (@i.o.scheffer on Instagram/author name: I.O. Scheffer), my editor, for being the author I've connected to most on Instagram, and for all the exchanges we've had. Thank you for offering to read my book and helping me to fix my grammatical and stylistic errors around dialogue, punctuation, and repetitive language. You're the reason I went back for my final edits, before deciding to bring you on as my editor. Above all, I wanted someone I trusted, and you're one of the people I trust most with my book. I will say that having you as an editor has been the best decision I've made for this book! You know exactly how to highlight the strengths in my writing. You've made my book much more accessible. You also offered feedback that allowed me to make several needed revisions. What feedback I didn't implement from you, I will most definitely keep in mind, while working on the rest of the series. This book would not be as good without you, and I have so much to thank you for. You're an amazing author who I look up to and respect. I love your books and would highly recommend them to any of my readers! They're some of the most meaningful books I've ever read, and they deserve to be read. I also want to thank you for your thoughts on neurodivergence regarding my characters (see "A Note on Neurodivergence").

Honestly, I came to realize I was using too much flowery and repetitive language. In the end, I trimmed my book down by 1,000+ words. Yes, it was that overdone. It also helps that I wrote my sequel between publishing delays, which gave me time to improve and think on my writing and feedback.

Above all, can I just say how delicately beautiful my cover art is! I just can't stop looking at it! Sophia Lindstrom did such an amazing job, and I can't imagine anything better. She's an amazing artist, and you can find her on her Instagram (@sophia.lindstrom.art). I am so incredibly grateful that I chose her to work with for this project, and I've loved working with her! She's added so much to this cover art that I wouldn't have thought of, and she perfectly understood the look and feel it should have, from concept to final artwork.

Lastly, I want to thank myself, because sometimes we need to. I want to thank myself for letting myself grow, heal, and be a kinder, more empathetic person. I want to thank myself for learning to love myself and grow into a more beautiful person, away from that suffocating pain and emptiness. I want to thank myself, now that I have self-worth, and confidence in this book that is my passion, and that I poured my heart into—and in myself. I want to thank myself for living, and to be able to give whatever kindness I can back in this book. Sometimes we need to be cradled by our own selfish wishes. And I hope you all keep reading and growing with Liela, Dunet, and Myllia, blossoming into kinder, more empathetic people that can bring beauty and love to this world.

Caroline Sophia Hamel

Discussion of Part 1

I want to save most of my discussion for when the final part is done. But I do want to say that this book is personal to me and holds the very depths of my heart. I always loved the emotion that stories made me feel. I love to cry more than anything, and have those emotions touch me deeply. If I can give any of that back and help anyone else grow, I want to.

This series is about growing with the people you love, about loving yourself, accepting and showing your vulnerability, letting go of your insecurities that hold you back, and finding self-worth, a reason to live, and a future that shines brightly ahead of you. More than anything, this is an optimistic book meant to cradle your heart and hold you close, to let you cry and know that it is okay ... To let you be the most beautiful person you can be.

Each of these characters I hold dearly to my heart. Liela has compassion, confidence, is extremely committed and dedicated to everything that she does, and has a steady drive forward for the people she cares about. But her insecurities equally hold her back. And she has an ambition and outlook that can seem almost child-like at times. She has so many sides to her, both warm and soft and rigid, confident, determined ... and she represents, most of all, the struggle and acceptance of my identity and self-expression. I subconsciously explored and processed much of my gender identity, sexuality, and self-expression through her character. She was a gateway to start understanding myself. She goes through a steady struggle between holding her dreams and growing with people she loves, holding her heart steady and unwavering through it all. I may not have always show this confident side, but I have been growing into it, as I've been becoming more myself.

Myllia is my timidness and absentmindedness—frozen in all her potential. But when she really wants something, she can put all her heart into it without hesitation. She is a hopeless, idealistic romantic, who pours her heart into books. She represents my romantic side and the love I read about and wanted to feel more than anything for much of my life. This is when I had no self-worth, and a need to find a reason to struggle forward in the search for love in another person. She is kind, even if her words are not always right, but she tries. She is a form of kindness I have witnessed so many times, and she has the kindness and patience I want to be able to express to others. Her arc is set to come in part 2, but everything is set up for her in part 1 to embrace her strengths. Just a bit of clarification, but Myllia *is* fat, and I meant for her to be read and represented that way. And to those of you who are fat/plus size, I hope you were able to see a healthy and positive depiction of yourselves. I'm not plus-size myself, so I appreciate any feedback on how I represented her.

Dunet is all my self-hate, lack of self-worth, and also my confidence—she has none of it, but she puts up a front, wanting to appear happy and to bring a smile to everyone's faces, but it cannot be truly genuine and meaningful until she embraces everything that she is. Dunet has anxiety and depression. She is drowning in her self-hate and utterly empty, suffocating, and lonely. She wants so much, but she doesn't know how to have it all without breaking her image. She's so afraid of that that she bottles everything in. She internalizes every little thing that she does wrong as they stack up and crush her. But she just wants to be the person she thinks everyone wants her to be. Her journey will be one towards self-love.

I did cut two characters and my old ending, but I acknowledged that I need to tell a better story and give a more optimistic conclusion. These two characters are Stell and Mirel ... and I hold them just as closely to my heart.

This story centers Liela and Dunet as the most important emotional conflict, of growing with each other and within ourselves to heal across gaps and in our own hearts. Much of what is in this book mirrors my own emotional growth, relationships, and emotional conflicts, even and long before I realized it myself ... Liela and Dunet's relationship specifically mirrors that between my mom and me, as we both learned to grow together. I was a very fragile person, like Dunet ... But there's much more that mirrors everything I have learned and held dear, and I hope to pass that to you and explore all the depths and inner turmoil of my characters as they learn to heal.

To leave one last note here, leading into the following parts:

For those of you with no self-worth, self-love, or confidence, like Dunet ... I hope you can rebuild and heal yourself alongside her.

For those of you drifting through life with no purpose, but so much kindness and so much to give, like Myllia ... I hope you can find something that brings you peace and creates a kinder world alongside her.

For those of you like both Liela and Dunet, who try too hard not to hurt each other and don't share yourselves or grow together ... I hope you can find genuine trust and love, to be able to move into a place of healing, and create genuine relationships that let you heal and learn and grow from one another alongside them.

For those of you like Liela, who have reached your dream but still scatter parts of yourself to the wind ... I hope you can find and embrace every part of yourself and never let yourself be constrained by the boxes you're put in.

To those of you who are LGBTQ+, I hope to continue writing stories you can see yourself in. I wish I had these stories earlier, so I could accept myself for who I am. I will continue writing these stories for you and for me, and I have expanded my exploration of identity in the sequel. You are not alone, and I love you.

For those of you who feel alone ... I believe everyone has kindness and that one day someone will see yours and love you for who you are, as long as you let yourself be that person for them, for yourself, and for the world.

I hope you continue reading and following the beauty of these three heroines, as they grow into beautiful, kinder people. Part 2 is scheduled to come out in late 2022. You can follow these websites and accounts for more details:

Website	carolinesophiahamel.com
Business Email	caroline@carolinesophiahamel.com
Instagram	@to_hold_a_flower (Caroline Sophia Hamel)
goodreads	Caroline Sophia Hamel

**I've added an additional note on neurodivergence on the following page. I'll likely include a longer discussion on neurodivergence in my sequels.

A Note on Neurodivergence

I recently started self-identifying as neurodivergent (an umbrella term for mental disabilities like autism, ADHD, and bipolar disorder). This was something that I accepted around the time of publication, so I didn't intentionally write any characters as neurodivergent. Still, I think it's important that I share this with you, in case you relate. I believe that a few of the characters in this novel are either neurodivergent or have neurodivergent traits. I intend to write Liela as a strongly masking autistic character and to incorporate that into her character arc (which will likely include her learning to unmask). I consider Liela canonically autistic.

Kreenie is also a character I now view as autistic and / or as having ADHD, and who doesn't mask her neurodivergence. I want to clarify that how she acts isn't wrong and I apologize if any of my readers felt like I treated her that way. As someone who masks my neurodivergence by people pleasing and following rules, her ability to not care is off-putting to me, but I now see it as freeing and positive. I realize several characters look down on or judge her for things she can't control (including Dunet). I want to reassure anybody with autism / ADHD that I don't intend to change her to act neurotypical. I plan to have her neurodivergence be embraced by the other characters.

And Dunet has several traits and experiences that I believe are neurodivergent traits. That said, I'm not sure whether I wrote enough of these traits into her to consider her canonically neurodivergent, or if she's just socially awkward. This depends on where I take her character. If you relate to her as neurodivergent, that's valid.

About the Author

Hello! My name is Caroline Sophia Hamel and my pronouns are she/her! I am a pansexual* transgender** girl and 22 years old. I also recently started self-identifying as neurodivergent (an umbrella term for mental disabilities). Being able to show all these wonderful emotions is my dream—to be able to have people feel and become kinder people.

I love emotional media that can make me cry. Bittersweet stories that make me simultaneously cry and smile are my favorite types of stories. While I used to love tragedy, hopeful stories now mean much more to me. As someone who's struggled with my identity and mental health, I understand that hope is what many of us need.

I'm an introverted girl who's building her confidence. Being on hormones has allowed me to feel much more myself.

I've had to go on my own journey to find self-love and healing. The world has become a much brighter place and I am glad to still be here, even if it's hard sometimes. I hope that I can help some of you heal. My goal is to help you find love within yourself, to grow your self-worth, and help you accept your strengths and all parts of yourself. Sometimes we feel far too broken, but when we mend, it's all worth it. Someday, I know that you'll love yourself.

If I can help anyone with my writing, then it's worth it.

I hope to show that there is light and beauty in life, just as there is darkness, and that we can embrace both and be whole.

Love to you all,

Caroline Sophia Hamel (she/her)

*Pansexual - Attracted to all genders

**Transgender (trans) – My gender doesn't match the one assigned to me at birth

-

If you would like to leave a review, it helps my reach a lot and I would very much appreciate it. Anyway, it means the world to share these characters with you! Part 2 is very far along at the time of writing this and I look forward to sharing it with you! You can find the synopsis on the following page.

The Essence of Longing

(To Hold a Flower Part 2)

Coming Late 2022 / Early 2023

~

As Liela deals with the realization that she no longer knows how to be there for Dunet, Dunet slowly isolates herself and loses everything that held her together. Liela desperately leans into others, trying to hold her world together, while Myllia works towards finding who she is as her relationship with Liela blossoms around their support for one another, and they both struggle to move forward. And throughout Liela's turmoil, she's still set on holding off the rising threat from the north, as the city's time runs out.

Caroline Sophia Hamel

Caroline Sophia Hamel